Praise for
OFFERINGS

"*Offerings* is a beautifully wrought coming-of-age story of a young man torn between art and commerce, conscience and obligation, Korea and the United States. I loved it."

—Malcolm Gladwell, *New York Times* bestselling
author of *Talking to Strangers*

"A potent combination of a financial thriller and a coming-of-age immigrant tale, *Offerings* is a great book. A thoughtful and engrossing read."

—Gary Shteyngart, award-winning and *New York Times*
bestselling author of *Our Country Friends*

"Michael Kim writes with the authority of an insider on the intricate workings of Wall Street and the high stakes for Korea during the Asia Financial Crisis, but at its core *Offerings* is a moving love story—about a young man's love for his home country, his father, and his newfound soul mate. *Offerings* is an elegant poem on the redemptive power of love."

—Sandy Weill, chairman emeritus of Citigroup
and bestselling author of *The Real Deal:
My Life in Business and Philanthropy*

"In clean, elegant prose, Michael Kim plumbs the complicated world of international finance—and the universal longing of fathers and sons not to disappoint one another. *Offerings* is the engrossing tale of an immigrant's troubled return home."

—Elizabeth Cobbs, *New York Times* bestselling author of
The Hamilton Affair and *The Tubman Command*

"This is a brilliant novel about a critical turning point both in a man's life and in his country of origin. The author, who was born in South Korea but lived much of his childhood in New Jersey, writes with rare clarity and great authority about high finance, the concept of home, and, most importantly, lessons learned from and redemption achieved with a beloved father."

—Nick Lyons, professor of English, Hunter
College (retired),and bestselling author

"If you want a look at a world you have never seen and appreciate rock-ribbed drama, then *Offerings* is that surprising item, a book that is at once new and fascinating."

—Craig Nova, author of *The Good Son*

OFFERINGS

A NOVEL

MICHAEL BYUNGJU KIM

ARCADE PUBLISHING • NEW YORK

First Paperback Edition 2022

This is a work of fiction. Names, places, characters, and incidents are either the products of the author's imagination or are used fictitiously.

Lyrics from "Morning Dew" by Min Ki Kim, copyright © 1971 by Min Ki Kim, reprinted by the kind permission of the Korean Society of Composers, Authors and Publishers.

Arcade Publishing books may be purchased in bulk at special discounts for sales promotion, corporate gifts, fund-raising, or educational purposes. Special editions can also be created to specifications. For details, contact the Special Sales Department, Arcade Publishing, 307 West 36th Street, 11th Floor, New York, NY 10018 or arcade@skyhorsepublishing.com.

Arcade Publishing® is a registered trademark of Skyhorse Publishing, Inc.®, a Delaware corporation.

Visit our website at www.arcadepub.com.
Visit the author's site at www.offeringsbook.com.

10 9 8 7 6 5 4 3 2 1

Library of Congress Cataloging-in-Publication Data is available on file.
Library of Congress Control Number: 2019957246

Cover design by Brian Peterson

ISBN: 978-1-956763-14-0
Ebook ISBN: 978-1-950691-69-2

Printed in the United States of America

To Abuji

OFFERINGS

The week before graduation, I told Abuji I was headed for Wall Street. The modern world, I said, as rehearsed, revolves around business, and its epicenter is Wall Street. It's Rome at the peak of the Roman Empire, the place to be for the best and brightest today.

"Where . . . what is Wall Street?" my father asked.

There are people in the world who have capital, I explained, and there are people who need capital. Investment bankers put them together. And, I mentioned, we get paid handsomely for it. I showed him the offer letter from Phipps & Co., presenting it like a winning lottery ticket.

Abuji took out his reading glasses and read the letter, slowly. When he was done, he said only, "Never been about money in Lee family." He was quiet for a long time. Then, "You're not going to get PhD?"

"Maybe later, Abuji," I said. And in the moment, I meant it.

He put his eyeglasses back in the breast pocket and calmly recited, in Korean, the long tradition of distinguished scholars in the Lee family, going back generations. Learning, wisdom, service, all his favorite themes, echoes from my childhood. He was too gentlemanly to cite then *sah-nong-gong-sang*, the prescribed Confucian social hierarchy: *sunbi* scholars at the top, followed by farmers, then artisans and, at the bottom, merchants—businessmen.

"Trust me," I wanted to tell Abuji. "For once, believe in your son. It's not giving in to mammon; I'm not selling out. I'm buying *in*. To this exciting new thing, even if it's not noble or high in the Confucian order, even though it's a road not taken by my ancestors. Or because it's not. I'm following my destiny, my own."

But there was too much in his face, the weight of years and illness, of expectation and hope and disillusionment. A father's judgment is a jagged stone in a stream, hard always but smoothed in the currents of time. I didn't argue. It would only have added to his confusion and disappointment. Time, I told myself, will make him understand.

I didn't know then time was one thing Abuji did not have. His mysterious illness would soon be diagnosed as pulmonary fibrosis. Like his father before him, Abuji would fall victim to the Lee family curse.

"I'll get to travel the world," I told him at the time. "Who knows, maybe even go back to Hanguk." He looked blankly at me.

Years later, this would come to pass. All the half-truths I told Abuji about Wall Street and being a merchant came to be realized, long after I had stopped believing them. I found myself, through

2

that bright miracle of chance that shines on the world, in the right place at the right time. A time of national crisis and reckoning. I served our homeland. And my own destiny blossomed, rock flower-like, through it all. But was it too late for him and me? For real resolution, reconciliation perhaps, or at least acceptance?

That is the question I ask myself even today, as I stand on our family mountain, Eunsan, outside of Seoul, holding my son's small hand. I take a deep breath and, together with my *jangnam*, kneel on the damp ground and do a ceremonial bow to Abuji and all the ancestors before him.

I

Oh, East is East, and West is West, and never the twain shall meet,
Till Earth and Sky stand presently at God's great Judgment Seat;
But there is neither East nor West, Border, nor Breed, nor Birth,
When two strong men stand face to face,
Tho' they come from the ends of the earth!

Rudyard Kipling, "The Ballad of East and West"

1

On a snowy day fifteen winters ago, I came home.

Asia was in crisis, and I came to save Korea. Land of my birth, home of my ancestors, my *gohyang*.

We touched down early at Gimpo, dawn uncurling its rosy fingers outside. "Welcome to the Land of Morning Calm," the PA said. Snow fell lightly; a blanket of white covered the *giwa* rooftops of the houses lining the runway.

They had told me in New York to pack my bags for Seoul, saying, "You are Korean, aren't you?"

There was a low hum at the airport. Visitors shuffling in line, officers tapping keyboards, bags circling on the carousel. Beneath it all, a stillness. The stillness of my childhood that used to fill our classrooms. When we were taught to be quiet, and not move. Words unspoken, thoughts unexpressed.

7

The officer at Passport Control looked from the eagle on my blue passport to me. "*Koondae?*" he asked. Military duty.

When I was twelve, I asked my father why we had decided to immigrate to the United States. "For your and your *dongseng's* education," he said, tousling my hair. One night, Abuji came home, Chivas on his breath, and he told me, "Today, you're naturalized, an American citizen. So you will not grow up to be one of them," he said. "Never serve in That Dictator's army."

I shook my head. "American," I told the officer. Wordlessly, he stamped my passport, waved me through.

One day back in Seoul, I came home from school to see Abuji standing by a small fire in the backyard of our house. He was burning a bundle of clothes. I could make out his officer uniforms, once so crisp, now a wrinkled heap, throwing off black smoke. I saw the medals of honor glow, then burn in the embers. I knew Abuji's job had been in the army, in intelligence. Through the smoke, I could make out tears running down his face. It was the first time I saw my father cry.

I made my way through the arrivals area, where there were not many people. There was no one to greet me.

"Home is where you start from," Abuji said, when he came to see me off at Kennedy Airport. "Over twenty years since we left, but it's still your *gohyang*." His face looked suddenly aged, already weak from disease, but the light there still. The light of a will to struggle, against his illness, and time. "Just need to keep breathing," he said, tapping his frail chest.

Outside, the morning fog rose, dissipated with the distant rumble of jets flying into the sky. On the Olympic Highway, the snow started to fall again, lightly, the thickening white carpet punctured by green bristles of rice plants.

The air felt heavy, as though weighed down with the burden of history. I felt the tiredness of the long flight. I rolled down the window in the taxi, and I saw snowflakes descend silent, and soft, and slow, Longfellow's poem of the air, revealing the secret of despair, and I thought of the centuries of foreign invasions of Korea, the colonial occupation by Japan, the Korean War, pitting brother against brother, leaving two countries at war still, a people divided. The long Han River snaked along beside us. I imagined the spirits from the war roaming the hills of Namsan and the ghosts of the tortured dissidents haunting the Blue House, where Park Chung Hee launched the headlong prosperity drive that produced the Miracle on the Han. All the ghosts of the past. I felt light-headed, fatigue creeping over my body. The tenth-wealthiest nation in the world, now on the brink of a sovereign default. I closed my eyes and held my breath in. I waited for my consciousness to dissolve.

I was back home, where I started.

2

Destiny, its seeds sown in the weepy rice paddies and dusty textile mills of a small, poor but big-dreaming country in the 1960s, has brought me by way of Wall Street to the banquet room of the Koryo Hotel. Four folding tables have been arranged into a neat rectangle. I sit with the rest of the Phipps & Co. working group at one long table; across from us is the team from Sterling Brothers. Two dozen knights in Savile Row armor, Mont Blanc swords drawn, ready for battle. There are no windows, no sunlight, just the heater going full blast. Like the heaters in the winters of my childhood. Koreans love their heat.

"Lookee all the muckety-mucks," whispers Jun, an associate from the Phipps Seoul office. He has tidy, closely cropped hair, but a cowlick sticks up in the back, making him look younger than he is. "Must be something big."

"Something *sexy*," Jack chimes in. "A merger with North Korea maybe. Better yet, a hostile takeover." Jack is a Corporate Finance vice president from New York. We were in the same associate training class when we became drinking buddies. His real name is Heathcliff Walker III, but his Cottage House brethren took to calling him Jack, short for Jackhammer (of a pair with his girlfriend, the Slab).

Jack has a sense, as we all do, of why we're here. Korea is in a financial meltdown. The Thai baht has already collapsed. Indonesia is effectively bankrupt. They're starting to call it the Asian Financial Crisis. Korea has been downgraded by Moody's to Baa3, borderline investment grade. Its stock market has plunged by 40 percent. The won in free fall. Three of the largest banks have gone under; several leading chaebol groups are rumored to be next. These family-owned conglomerates dominate Korean business, and the fate of the economy is tied to their survival. We, the Phipps and Sterling bankers, have been sent from New York to work out a rescue package for Korea. Before the contagion spreads across Asia, and beyond.

As we take our places, beepers go off, in a chorus of chirps and buzzes. News flash on BlackBerries: *Kim Dae Jung projected to win the Blue House.* DJ, as he's known, is a reform-minded liberal, and his presidential victory will be the first by an opposition candidate in the brief history of free elections in Korea. As a dissident under the Park Chung Hee regime, DJ was tortured by the Korean CIA:

he still has a limp in his walk to show for it. He is famous for having said in prison, "They can choke the rooster, but the sun will rise in the morning." He ran his campaign on a platform of a "sunshine policy" toward North Korea. He advocates warming the North with sunny policies of engagement rather than the historical approach of blowing harsh, cold sanctions at them. People say he's either after a Nobel Peace Prize or a closet Communist.

We look up from our devices as a tall, wiry man strides into the room. He's in his midfifties, sports wire-rim glasses. A man in tow, half a foot shorter, announces, "The Minister of Finance and Deputy Prime Minister of the Republic of Korea."

The Koreans rise to their feet, and the rest of us follow, a bit uncertainly.

The minister takes off his glasses, wipes the lenses on his tie, rubbing small concentric circles. "Gentlemen," he says. "Our country is in crisis." The minister speaks in a barely audible voice, forcing us to concentrate on his words. He is used to being center stage.

"The Big Dawg," Jack mutters.

"All that's standing between him and the Blue House is a miraculous economic recovery," Jun adds.

The man trailing Choi intones, "What honorable minister is saying is our country is in, how you say, desperate measure." Yoon is director-general at the Ministry of Economy and Planning, MoEP for short. He has dyed jet-black hair, and his furtive, eager-to-please glances at the minister betray a career bureaucrat. "Foreign reserves of our great country are down to US dollar fifty billion." He pauses, counts off the zeros on his sheet again, corrects: "I mean US dollar five billion." He turns to the assistant behind his shoulder, who nods in approval of his superior's zero-counting prowess.

"Country going *down*," Jack says under his breath.

"If we do not find a solution to current problem," says Choi, still barely above a whisper, "our country will be . . . bankrupt." He scans the room, seems to zoom in on me. "It is up to you, the best and brightest in world of finance, to save our country from ruin."

"Your two most venerable houses have been called here," Yoon adds, "to advise government of Korea on development and execution of a financing strategy." He takes his jacket off, revealing braided leather suspenders with clip-ons, and rolls up the shirtsleeves, his short arms requiring only two skinny revolutions of fabric. "Now, let's get down to *bidness*."

The government officials share a seriousness and a sense of duty, a sacred condition that holds them aloft, pulled down only by anxiety and panic from the imminent peril facing their country. Glory will be theirs presently, if they could just get over this economic crisis.

First to speak is the silver-haired senior banker from Sterling. Gandalf the Grey —a nickname he bestowed on himself and enforces among his colleagues—came from the State Department, where he was assistant deputy undersecretary of state. Or rather, Gandalf opens his mouth to speak with a loud "Ahem," but he's cut off by his counterpart from Phipps, Ignatio—a.k.a. The Monkey. The Monkey has a round face with features slightly off center, like a reflection in a spoon. He also has a beard, uncommon among bankers, which has declared war on the entire face, threatening to conquer the last bare epidermal holdouts, nose and eyelids. The Monkey is a figure of respect and revulsion, known equally for his deal savvy and his abusive treatment of subordinates. Unlike Gandalf, he is never called by his nickname.

"What we have here," the Monkey squeaks in his distinctive high pitch, "is a perception problem, not an economic fundamentals problem." He waves a hairy hand for emphasis: "Let's not forget, Korea is still the tenth-largest GDP in the world, with growth rates of—"

"At the end of the day, though, it's really a credit problem," Gandalf rumbles in the rich baritone on which he prides himself, the voice of experience and wisdom. "Gentlemen, we must engage posthaste with the rating agencies in re the current . . . situation. We at Sterling Brothers would be happy to take the lead, given that the head of our credit department is the former head of Moody's Sovereign Ratings—"

"First things first," the Monkey interrupts. A partner in the last privately held firm on Wall Street, he's asserting his natural superiority over a managing director from a publicly traded house. "It's not credit per se. It's credibility. First thing we do, we assess the reputational damage to Korea in the international markets. Only *then* can we start to think about restoring—"

Minister Choi has been sitting still, eyes closed. He clears his throat. "Allow me to be clear. We brought in Phipps and Sterling to be coadvisors to government of Korea." He looks at Gandalf,

then the Monkey. "Equal billing. So I'll expect you to be cooper-
ative and work . . . collegially with each other."

He's handed a note. The furrowing of his eyebrows suggests
something from the Blue House, maybe the president-elect. The
bankers around me don't seem to notice—they're already deep in
negotiations of their own.

A Sterling MD: "Can we assume we'll be the sole global joint
lead advisers? We can bring in co-'s later, but you can't have too
many chefs in the kitchen."

A Phipps ED, nodding his agreement: "Can't have all chiefs
and no Indians."

My hand rises. To say what? That this is a deal that is more
than a transaction, what Abuji might call *chun-jae il-woo*, a once-
in-a-thousand-years opportunity? An opportunity to stare dark
destiny in the face and defy it, in a put-our-foot-down statement
for humanity? If we pull this off, it will be a shining, noble achieve-
ment, something to tell our grandchildren. I can see myself in a
rocking chair: "Your *halabuji* saved the motherland from ruin!" So,
for once, let's stop with the penis measuring and all pitch in! Then
I remember Abuji telling me, "The riper the rice plant, the more it
bows its head." I slowly lower my hand.

A Sterling MD pipes up. "What about our . . . the fee?"

Ah, the magic word. We investment bankers like to think
we're a breed apart, sharper, *better* than everyone else. We perpetuate a self-mythology of a master race that controls the destiny of the world. There's a fine line, of course, between a vision
and a delusion. At my Phipps job interview, I made the mistake

of asking the French-cuffed, Hermès tie–clad VP interviewing me, "So, what's the difference between i-bankers and commercial bankers?"

"First," he sniffed, "we don't call ourselves 'i-bankers,' and, second, we outwork, outsmart, um, out-*tough* everyone else. We look for the kind of guys who wake up in the morning ready to bite the ass off a bear. That's what we're paid so handsomely for." I fought off the vision of his Hermès tie dangling between the shaggy legs of a grizzly.

What motivates bankers, the single, crystal driver, is money; it *defines* them. Green, dough, moola, filthy lucre. The holy year-end bonus. But we never talk about money; it's beneath us. We bring it up only when we have to.

The room goes quiet, a heavier hush than before.

The minister looks up and stares at the MD from Sterling.

"I mean, it's a huge assignment," the banker says, meekly. "It'll require a globally coordinated team effort, from Credit to Corp Fin to Capital Markets to Fixed Income."

"Gentlemen, I've just been summoned," the minister says, "by the Blue House, I believe for a briefing on the current economic situation. But please know that the president will not take office for two months." A pause. "By then, our country may have collapsed. For now, I'll leave our fate in your capable hands."

Everyone stands as he leaves the room.

Yoon takes his cue. "Be so kind as to settle in, gentlemen," he says. "We are going to be all night." With a flourish, he pulls out a black binder two inches thick. "Our latest economic indicators."

He slams another binder, even thicker, on the table. "Our financial sector statistics."

Gandalf and the Monkey and several of the other senior bankers take this as their cue to go. "You don't mind if we excuse ourselves," Gandalf murmurs. "You're in good hands with our—"

"Yes, I mind," Yoon says, without looking up. "Please sit," motioning with his hand.

The MDs are caught in limbo, up from their seats but not pushed off from the table. They float, then subside.

Out of the corner of my eye, I see Jack suppressing a grin.

Beyond him, I see a red EXIT sign over the door. There's a red stick figure, looking to run, away somewhere.

A crisis, a remembrance, a destiny unspooling. I feel OK, I tell myself, despite the jet lag, and the heat, maybe even getting a second wind. I take a deep breath and hold it. An old habit from when I was growing up. When I stop breathing, the world drifts away, time stands still. I once went four minutes without exhaling. I saw somewhere that *Jeju haenyuh*, women sea divers, can hold their breath underwater for twelve minutes on a dive. I close my eyes, imagine I'm a little boy again seeing how long he can hold his breath.

3

May 1976

I am Korean. My name Dae Joon, mean Big Hero, and I come from Seoul, big city in my country. Family come to New Jersey in America because Father say America good for my education. Education important to Appa. America land of opportune, he say. Also land of brave, home of free. Also beautiful. I like sound, beauuuutiful, except American don't pronounce *t*. They say beauuu-leeful. *L* or *r* not sure, not *t*.

When Umma, little sister Dongseng, and me arrive in New Jersey, Appa has apartment. Pretty, very American. American curtain and bed, we not sleep on floor. My bed has blanket, green with racing car, little sister red blanket with cartoon dog Appa say Snoopy. Like American home. But I sleep in room with sister because only two bedroom. She scared at night, big tree outside window move branch, like ghost. Say she want to go home. Umma say, "Shhhh, Ttal, we are home."

People very different in new country. They look different, all different color hair, why so many different color? They talk different, never say sound *t*, all *l* and *r*. They even smell different. Umma say they smell like *bbaddah*, butter, or maybe cheese.

My first day at Eagle Stone Elementary School, Appa change my name because American cannot say Dae Joon. Don't know why, so simple. My new name Shane. Appa like the American cowboy movie, and Shane famous American cowboy. He say I sound American, like cowboy. I like my real name, not American cowboy name.

I tell new classmate I am from Korea, and they don't know. They say I look Chinee or Japanee. I tell them my country has Kim Il, pro wrestler world champion. They say who? I cannot know why they do not know Kim Il. Most fearsome wrestler, and from my country. He throw people easy and hit their head with his head to make their head bloody. They say does he know karate? Then they kick feet and they make noise, *huyyaaa, whooeee*. They look like crazy monkey, make loud noise. Different from classmate in my country.

I like food in this country. Umma take Dongseng and me to supermarket, not just market, where there is so much food. I like word *super*—Superman, Super Bowl, supermarket. Super-duper! America also land of plenty. So much of everything. I like ice cream most. Cold window in supermarket has many ice cream in the vanilla, strawberry, chocolate. Breyers chocolate my best. No ice cream back home. Umma say ice cream good because milk in it, and milk good for you, make you tall, like American. So soft and melting slow on my tongue, rolling around, cold then cool then gone. I can eat ice cream every day. Why eat rice? Ice cream breakfast, ice cream lunch, ice cream dinner. Maybe vanilla in breakfast, strawberry lunch, and my best chocolate in dinner. Beauuuleeful.

In first days, my English talking not so good. I don't like opening mouth to speak at the school. Don't understand what smiling American teacher say. But Ms. Viden she nice, put her head down close to my head when she speak to me. She has gold hair, and she smell like the fake flower. Reading class I stay quiet. But math so easy. Numbers talk to me. Teacher ask me to divide 1920 by 16, I tell her from my head 120, then she ask me square root of 14,400, and I say 120 again, and she put me in seventh-grade math class next day.

Appa tell me learn English by reading book out loud. Why get the English tutor? he say. You read, you learn. So I read, every book loud. Sister enjoy me reading book. Dick and Jane went up the hill to fetch a pail of honey. Humpty Dumpty fell off truck. Umma go over vocabulary with me, make sure I learn fifty word a day she put on small index card with date at top. Airplane, apple, automobile, autumn. Chair, door, kitchen, television, also called TV. Why telephone not called TP? And why *W* called double *u*, not double *v*? Strange language, but I like sound.

First week at Eagle Stone, in recess Don Krieger call me Chink. First time I hear chink. Other kids laughing. I want to ask what it mean, chink, but I cannot say question. So I turn away. But he follow me, say, "Chicken Chink, Chicken Chink, *quoak, quoak.*" He pump elbow up and down, then he push me. I give him roundhouse kick to stomach, just like in tae kwon do class. He make noise like *pffffff,* both leg bend, and he fall to ground, *thud.* He cry, loud. Kids laugh at him now. I think I should laugh, too, but I feel sad inside. Ms. Viden come then and take me away before somebody see tear on my face.

She put arm on my shoulder and say, "You have to be strong. You're in America now."

*

In day, Umma cook food and sing old Korean song *"Arirang"* and some other sad song I know but don't know name. In night before sleeping, she tell me and Dongseng many old Korean folk story. So we don't forget our homeland, she say. She tell story about tiger, turtle, fox, and sometimes ghost. Dongseng not like tale of ghost. Sometime after the ghost story she cannot sleep.

My best is about boy who love story so much he collect many good story in small cloth pouch he carry at his belt. Every good story he hear he pack in pouch and close it up. Soon his pouch so full it about to bust, but he tie it even tighter so none of story get out. He go everywhere with story bag. People start noticing many strange sound coming out of pouch.

One day nosy grown-up man snatch pouch from boy and open it. Hundred garden snake hiss and crawl out from bag. Snake scare everyone and all crawl away. Boy is so sad because all his story leave him, after all that collecting and keeping.

Umma tell us that's why story meant not keep yourself but hear and tell other people. She say story are to share.

4

December 31, 1997

"What we are facing is not an economic crisis," Director Suh is saying. "It is a liquidity problem."

Suh is disheveled, in a way that announces he's got more important things on his mind than attire. He speaks nearly perfect, clipped English, honed while earning his PhD at the University of Illinois. He's the head of the international finance bureau and *team-jang* of the Financial Crisis Project Task Force Team, a multiagency task force, "PTFT" to the Koreans.

We're on the sixth floor of the MoEP, known fondly as "the Mop," in Gwacheon, a half hour outside of Seoul. Slabs of drab gray cinder blocks on the outside, paint peeling on the walls inside, linoleum floors, a few patches curling up at the edges; every table and chair aluminum. The lights are fluorescent, one occasionally sizzling, on, off, on.

The Mop guys on the PTFT are easy to tell from the others. Unlike the bankers, they have neat parts in their hair, combed, not brushed, and they wear short-sleeve dress shirts and ties. Even in winter, no doubt due to the heater going full blast, they wear short sleeves. But, more, they have, in the tradition of *sunbi*, the air of true believers. A poster on the wall reads: OUR DUTY IS OUR HONOR.

"More accurately, a short-term liquidity problem," he says. "Just get over this, uh, hump, and we shall be fine."

When he's sure he has everyone's attention, Suh goes to the whiteboard, the kind on wheels, and proceeds to draft a presentation for investors on the current situation. Suh is known as a *chil-bo ji-jae*, one of those court scholars of old who could compose a poem in seven steps. He recites as he writes, using no notes.

"Slide number one: Korea's GDP amount and year-on-year growth for the last twenty years, showing double-digit growth until 1997," he says. "Slide number two: Export growth of more than 12 percent CAGR over this same period."

He rolls up his sleeves. "Slide number three: Korea's foreign commercial debt, standing at twenty-four-point-five billion dollars, or 8.2 percent of GDP. Slide number four: Percentage of foreign debt due to mature in less than one year: 85 percent short-term debt to GDP."

Suh takes off his tie, tosses it on a chair.

"Slide number five: Principal plus interest due of fifteen billion dollars versus foreign reserves of five billion dollars." He turns to us. "If our country is downgraded by Moody's one more notch, we will face the shame of being the first industrialized nation to become a . . . *below-investment-grade credit.*"

"A sovereign junk credit," Jun points out, shaking his head. He twirls his pen on his hand like a helicopter blade, the way all Korean-educated people do.

Suh is about to recite his next slide, but again the Monkey ahems his way onto the floor. The Monkey is one of the few single partners at Phipps, and sightings of him in West Village bars have made the rounds and gained him some renown as a maverick on Wall Street. "We need to roll over the twenty-five billion dollars of foreign commercial bank debt owed by the Korean banks," he says, his voice even higher than usual. "The first thing we need to do is reschedule that debt."

"We shall support it," Suh says. "The government of our country is prepared to—"

At the back of the room, the door opens, and the crowd parts for a tall, overweight man in his midsixties, ruddy in his rumpled Brooks Brothers suit, trailed by a woman in her twenties. She's the only woman in the room, and her blonde hair makes her stand out even more. I recognize Tom Brogan, formerly chairman of the New York Federal Reserve, now vice chairman of Phipps International, a made-up division to put on his business card. I'd heard Brogan was called in by Minister

Choi, who knew him from their days working at the International Monetary Fund, for his sovereign bailout experience.

"Anybody here," he booms—no greeting, no introduction—"ever been through a national debt crisis?"

Thirty faces with blank expressions, a few looking at one another. Jack rolls his eyes.

"Well, I have."

"Here it comes," says Jack, under his breath.

"As chairman of the New York Fed, I oversaw the Latin American bailout of the eighties. Let me tell y'all what we need to do." Pause, for effect. "What we're going to do is exchange the banks' loans into government-guaranteed debt. A good ol' debt exchange offer. Not just a rollover by the banks, but the Korean government stepping up with a full guarantee. The government prepared to do that?"

All eyes turn to Director Suh.

"I shall need to brief the minister," Suh says. "If it is what is required—"

I look over his head at the TV monitor in the corner. News bulletin: North Korea has just launched a medium-range ballistic missile over the East Sea, known by non-Koreans as the Sea of Japan. The missile cannot reach the mainland United States, but Japan is well within its range.

Someone from Phipps says, "The international banks need to agree to the rollover if the government is willing to provide the—"

"We at Sterling were, of course, also involved in the Latin America bailout—"

"—view is that we should follow up the exchange offer immediately with an issuance of global sovereign bonds—"

"—new debt issued by the Government of Korea—"

"—critical to instill confidence in Korea in the international markets—"

"—shore up the depleted FX reserves—"

"—lest the markets turn their backs on the country and—"

"This latest act of provocation by the authoritarian Communist regime of Kim Jong Il is sure to—"

"Can we not issue through the Korea Industrial Development Bank?" Suh says. "They're the well-known credit in the Yankee bond and Eurobond markets . . ."

A still shot of Secretary-General Kim Jong Il comes on the screen, the Dear Leader in all his smiling, sun-glassed, perm frizz glory. Then the obligatory grainy black-and-white image of his father, the Eternal Leader Kim Il Sung. The elder Kim is in his EL pose, smiling and waving in full military regalia, with a banner behind him declaring, VICTORIOUS FATHERLAND LIBERATION WAR and, in smaller letters below it, OVER THE AMERICAN IMPERIALIST AGGRESSORS.

In my schooldays in Korea, we were made to draw posters as part of regular anti-Communism campaigns. I drew one in Cray-Pas of the Eternal Leader of the North as a red devil, with horns, pointy mustache, and a wickedly long tail. It was selected to represent our school in a nationwide contest. I have the medal to prove it.

"It has to be a sovereign bond, not quasi-sovereign. Full faith and credit of the government—"

"—In fact, we hear the state bank KIDB is planning a Yankee bond as we—"

"—we strongly suggest you pull—"

I read somewhere that North Korea's populace is down to food rations of one bowl of rice a day. Only soldiers in the People's Army get two bowls of rice. People in the countryside are so deprived of nutrition they're resorting to eating placenta left over from childbirths. For the protein and fats. Sometimes fried with onions, sometimes raw, placenta tartare. Maybe we should be doing a sovereign global bond offering for them, the starving people of North Korea. We could call it Placenta Bonds.

"This here offering needs to be large," Brogan says, his broad chest puffing up with his words. "Enough to make an impact. To the tune of ten billion or so, US. To have a dad-gum *impact*."

At mention of this number, everyone stops talking. A hush falls across the room; only the soft rattle of the heaters can be heard. I can almost see the tumblers turning in the bankers' heads as the fees are calculated. At 1 percent, our take would be one hundred million dollars. The Monkey clamps his lips to stifle a grin.

Brogan goes on: "We'll need to have our credit rating advisory team do a diligence session with the minister. We'll also need to interview the president-elect—"

Suh looks pained. "Afraid impossible." Arranging a meeting for your new boss to be grilled by foreign bankers is a career-shortening opportunity for a bureaucrat.

There are a few due-diligence questions I'd ask of the Dear Leader. Do you know what placenta tastes like? How do you retain your Rubenesque figure? Just between us, would you really bomb your fellow Koreans?

"Y'all want to save the country or not?" Brogan says, his pink face turning red.

"Right now, Moody's and S&P have you by the short hairs," the Monkey says, helpfully. "You get downgraded, your interest rate goes up by up to four-to-five hundred basis points. If you can even place the bonds—"

"You either play ball or we can all go—"

Poor Director Suh. He's overmatched. The old Wall Street tools of fear and intimidation at work. The banks always have more information than their clients. "Info asymmetry" is the term of art. And they're not afraid to use it to their advantage. Whether the information is relevant, or even accurate, is beside the point.

"What about North Korea? We'll need to assess the geopolitical risk on the Peninsula—"

We're interrupted by uniformed female assistants bringing in *doshirak*. They appear quietly and place one boxed lunch in front of each banker. Each *doshirak* contains braised beef and is brimming with seasoned vegetables, and white rice and kimchi, of course. I think, it must also be lunchtime in Pyongyang.

Brogan scowls at the box in front of him. "Jesus H. Christ," he growls. "How 'bout some REAL food?!"

The assistants stand stricken with terror, but Brogan's blonde assistant gives them a reassuring nod as she scurries out the door in search of a McDonald's.

The Sterling MD turns to a younger colleague, says under his breath, "Where the hell is Gandalf?"

Gandalf apparently doesn't like to be present when Brogan is headlining a meeting. And vice versa. Every bigwig needs his space.

"What say we get started on drafting the preliminary prospectus?" the Monkey says. "Leading the way on the Red Herring will be our own DJ Lee." He crooks a long, hairy finger in my direction. "He's Korean, by the way."

*

It's past midnight, and the bustle and noise in the Mop offices have been replaced by an undulating quiet. The quiet echoes off the concrete walls, the fluorescent lights flickering, like candles in a gentle wind.

Jack and I are the last ones remaining from the PTFT, and Jack's head is buried in his arms on the aluminum table. Torn Post-its and half-written pages on Korea's creditworthiness are scattered about his head. A wave of fatigue washes over me, and I force myself to get up from the table, take a walk.

Out the window, past my own reflection, I see a near-full moon and frost on the tree branches. I press my face against the windowpane. My breath fogs up the glass under my cupped hand, then the fog-flake fades, one capillary at a time.

I walk down the hallway past the dark rooms and, here and there, a light. I pass a room where Director Suh, shirttail out, is reading notes off an index card—rehearsing his next impromptu performance. He enunciates each English word, repeating the difficult ones over and over. *Liquidity, sovereign, bailout, li-QUI-dity.*

I can barely keep my eyes open. At the end of the corridor I see a dark room and duck inside, thinking maybe I can catch a nap. Through the dark, I see first the orange ember of a cigarette, sizzling as it's sucked. My eyes adjust, and I make out Minister Choi, leaning against a wall in front of an open window, cigarette held in his long fingers. He still has his suit jacket on.

As I turn on my heels to leave, the minister calls after me, softly, "Lee *Yisa*, isn't it? From Harvard?" *Hah-ba-deu*, three syllables.

I heard Minister Choi graduated number one in his class at Seoul National Law. Recorded the highest civil service exam score in history, went on to obtain the obligatory PhD from the Kennedy School of Government. Rumor has it he has an eidetic memory and can recite entire passages from *I Ching*.

"HBS," I say, adding, ". . . sir. I went to Swarthmore undergrad."

If the clarification registers, he doesn't show it. "I enjoyed immensely my years in Cambridge," he says, staring out the window. He stubs out his cigarette in a plastic cup, lets out one final spiral of smoke through his nostrils. "We appreciate all your hard work," he says. "Your country appreciates it." He speaks English carefully but mellifluously, his words strokes of calligraphy.

I move closer, and I see the youthful face I saw earlier in the day, but with purple crescents underneath his eyes and stubble flecked with silver on his chin.

He asks about my family, switching to Korean. Where my father is from and where he went to school. He thinks they must have overlapped somewhere. He asks whether I'm single. I tell him I am, and he nods in approval.

The minister takes off his eyeglasses, holds them up in the moonlight. "We will get through this," he says. "Through discipline and hard work, as we always do." He adds, with conviction, "We Koreans outwork everybody."

"*Neh, Jangkwannim,*" I say, nodding as respectfully as I know how.

"But we must do it our way," he says. "Lee *Yisa*, they teach you at Harvard about the virtues of free markets? US model of laissez-faire capitalism. The final form, the end of history." He pauses. "What they do not tell you is that it is not universally applicable. They frown on any central planning done by ministries like ours. Make fun of our five-year economic plans. What they do not realize is the 'invisible hand' in markets Adam Smith talks about is . . . us." Another pause. "The Ministry of Economic Planning is the hand that guides the economy and markets behind the scenes.

"You see, one cannot just pluck a plant from American soil and transplant it in Asia and expect it to flourish," he says. "Different soil, different water, even sunlight. One must adapt it to local conditions. As Singapore President Lee Kuan Yew said of democracy, Asians must develop an Asian model of democracy, not just copy Western liberal democracy. One prioritizing group harmony over individual liberty. So we need to develop our own model of capitalism. *Asian* capitalism."

He continues in his soft monotone; I try to keep up with his Korean. "Individual greed is not good, corporate layoffs are destructive to society. Free markets, yes, but with some guidance from the people who . . . know more, who have wisdom."

He lights another cigarette. Marlboro, Abuji's brand. The fragrance of my childhood.

The minister tells me about the Confucian order of society. Ruler takes care of subjects, teacher imparts knowledge to pupils, and civil servants run society. *Sunbi* study their entire lives to pass the civil service exam for that privilege, which is really a right. That's the way it's always been, over the millennia. The old Asian way. Even in the West, the guardians Plato talks about run Kallipolis. *We* are the philosopher-kings, he tells me. I nod politely, and I look over his shoulder at the poster on the wall, reading, WE SERVE THE PUBLIC.

Now he's describing Asians' natural intellectual-cultural-moral superiority. Asia, led by China, the Middle Kingdom, so named because it's the center of the universe, dominated all of human history except for the last one and half centuries. Think about it, he says, pacing. Shadows ripple across his face in the faint moonlight. All important advances in human endeavor were made in China. From philosophy and art to invention of paper and compass and clock to even noodles. Just one thing the West has been better at: the application of science to military purposes. Barbarians in the West just make more destructive weapons. That is the basis of US hegemony, despite American society's lack of morals or even moral knowledge.

I try to concentrate on what he's saying, but his words bleed together, his voice grows fainter.

I remember reading of a great Confucian scholar celebrated for his deep knowledge of all subjects. At thirty, he was said to have mastered the classics, mathematics, astronomy, and medicine as well as seven foreign languages. A faithful student of Confucius, he could recite at will the teachings on reverence for elders and filial piety. He had what Taoists called *he-an pang-kwang*, spiritual eye-distant vision, and became widely known as a seer. People said he was able to see events in distant lands and predict things to happen in the future.

The scholar became so famous for his wisdom that one day Confucius called for him and took him up the Tai Mountains overlooking the On kingdom. There at the peak, Confucius asked the younger man what he saw. The disciple replied, "I see nine white horses tied at the gates of On."

To which Confucius said, "No, your vision is imperfect. What you see is not white horses but rolls of white silk hung out for bleaching." He added, "Desist your seeing."

When I realize the Minister has stopped talking, I thank him for the lecture. "*Kamsahapnida*," I mumble. "For enlightening me."

"When this is all over, Lee *Yisa*," he says, putting a hand on my shoulder. "You must return here. Serve your homeland."

"*Neh.*"

"Maybe settle down . . . with a nice Korean girl. I might even know someone suitable."

I nod, *Neh* again, and as I walk back to my desk, the sweet, bitter smell of Marlboros still in my nostrils, I wonder, *Can you return to a place you never really knew?*

5

June 1976

I was born one year old.

In my country, you are one year at birth. How can you be zero year old? You can't be nothing! And you eat one more year at beginning of year. Because new year. My new American friends ask me: So, if born on December 31, then in two days later, you're two years old? I never thought it that way. Americans sure think different. Or they don't like other ways of doing things.

My most early memory is Umma and me on city bus, so smelly of gasoline and loud noise, to Myung-dong. She take me to American ham-bug restaurant for cheeseburger and chocolate milkshake. They play the rock-and-roll music in restaurant. My first taste of America. Up to then, my only American taste the Spam, pink American meat given by neighbor who worked at US Army PX. Umma make Spam and egg sandwich for lunch *doshirak* for me. When I hold thick sandwich in my hands, juice from meat ooze out. Classmates in first grade wish they're me.

Umma made me take tae kwon do. "No one bully son of mine," she say. After one year of lessons, she take my hand to tae kwon do testing center and say may my son take *yoodanja* test? Official check record and say your son not ready for black belt. Umma bowed and ask again. When they turn away, she get down on both knee and give deep ceremonial bow, forehead on ground, what we do at family *jesa*. She not get up until they let me take test. I do advanced form and then they make me spar with another black belt test taker about my age. Soon as referee say go, kid fly to me with the flying side kick and both his feet land on my face. My face puffy and blue, but we walk out of testing center with shiny paper saying I'm black belt. I bring belt home to show Appa. I tell him they call me Tiger in *tae kwon dojang*, and he smile and say, "OK, Tiger."

*

In elementary school, called People's School in my country, we had anti-Communism education every week. Teacher say Communism bad, and North Korea started 6.25 War. Bad *ppalgengyi*, Reds, want to start another war. *Kanchup*, Red spies, all around us. We make posters showing Red devils with horns and saying if you see any, call 113, *kanchup* hotline. When I ask teacher why Reds want to attack us, she say because they want to steal our freedom. When I ask why they want to steal it, don't they have any of their own, she say Kim Il Sung is evil leader and take everything away. When I ask if kids in North have anti–South Korea education class, she get angry and make me write on chalkboard, "*Ppalgengyi* are our enemy," one thousand time.

In anti-Communism class, they show us scary pictures from 6.25 War. Teacher say we must be strong country, avoid another war like this. North soldiers in pictures all look evil and crazy. There's one picture of Red with red eyes stick a rifle with knife at end into mother from South with holding baby, and he shouting like he enjoy it. I have bad dream of hundred Reds who look just like him, all red eyes, attacking my home. They try to stick gun with knife in Umma and me. I have this bad dream many times.

When I ask Umma what was it like in War, she look away, not say anything. One day on bus ride we pass by small mountain near our home called Namsan, and Umma say that's where her parents are. I didn't know there are graves in Namsan. She say no graves but it's still graveyard. Her *umma* and *appa* are there in cave somewhere. She say she was little girl when War broke out, and she got separated from her parents there. One day she will go look for cave.

That night I ask about rest of her family. Umma say she had an *unni* and a twin sister. A twin—another Umma! It excite me so much I beg her tell me more more more. Did she look just like you? Were you two best friend? But she just say, she was separated

41

from her and her older sister too. I ask her many times, What happened? Were they also in the cave? She say, War happened to them. She doesn't say more, she just wipe her eyes.

Umma once showed me scar on her stomach from War. I imagine bad *ppalgengyi* shooting her with gun or even huge cannon. I touch the scar, and I feel something metal under skin. She say she carry War with her.

*

We lived in redbrick house in Sinchon, in old Seoul. We had front yard of dirt, and I play with friends there. It was only yard in neighborhood. There was *gahm* tree in middle. Per-simmon in English I learn. Every October maid noona and I stand on ladder and pick many ripe orange *gahm*. We say shoo to *ggachi* trying to eat them, though everyone say this bird bring good news. Noona like to kiss me on cheek when adults not looking.

One day I come from school to find no Noona and my pink plastic piggy bank split open in belly and all the coin gone. I spent years putting coin in pink piggy. I go cry to Appa, but he just say, "She needed it more." I never see Noona again.

We had no TV in our home, but I remember black piano in living room. Appa play for hours. Sound nice but mostly so sad. Dark room in back had many shelves full of the books. Lots of thick books and some old or paperback. They were Korean and Chinese books but also some English. Appa all the time alone in that room. His *sanctum sanctum*, I think he call it. He warn me not go play in there, not the playroom. But I think books full of stories, so why not fun? I thought authors are magician, use wand to put words together on paper and make stories, make characters. Just make them up out of imagination! And all different people read it. Is that not magic? I felt magic in that room.

When Appa went to university to teach, sometimes I go in his sanctum and look at books. All wonderful acts of magic. I could read some Korean books, but I like the way English books look. The English even smell different. They smell fresher than the dusty old Korean books. I touch my fingers on the pages of books and flip through, like I'm really reading. I like saying the fancy author names, Tho-reau, Fit-z-ge-ral-d, He-ming-wa-y, Jo-y-ce, Mel-ville, Faul-k-ner. All so foreign, like American. I imagine they live in different world, place where everyone tall, good, and happy. Always in the sunshine. Different from my country. And sure different from unfree North. I don't know what they write about in America if everyone all happy. Maybe write about how they can share the happiness with other people, like Koreans. That would really be magic.

When Appa tell me we move to America, I ask, So we can be tall and happy too? He say he'll go first and find out.

6

Early January 1998

"Our story," Hyun Suk says, "is the history of Korea Inc."

Hyun Suk, Wayne to me, has a leg draped across the arm of a red silk-covered chair, telling me, in his languid way, the illustrious corporate history of the Ilsung Group. We're in his private office, which is in a hotel, the Hotel Kukje, which is owned by Ilsung. When I entered the hotel lobby, which resembled a spaceship in a 1950s movie, a young woman, in a uniform of Ilsung blue, ushered me discreetly to a private elevator bank. The elevator used only by the Ilsung chairman and, they say with a snicker, *Wangjanim*. The Prince, Wayne Park. She bowed, pushed the PH button, and we rode up in swooshing silence.

Wayne and I met during our first year at Harvard Business School. We were not in the same section, but we were two of only a handful of Korean students our year, and our fathers had known each other during their *yuhak* days at George Washington. They had been the only Koreans at GW in those days. Abuji told me to look out for Wayne. I shared my case study notes with him. He took me to parties at Wellesley in his Carrera. He had a laugh that was unbridled mirth, a promise to bring you on an adventure. Wayne and I were both victims of our fathers' passion for American cowboy movies. Hence Shane and Wayne, after John Wayne. We had that in common, and it became our little running joke. We took to calling each other "pardner."

Wayne shares the penthouse floor with his father, the group chairman. There are a Pollock and a Lichtenstein, featuring a blonde woman with a thought bubble—*THAT'S WHAT WE SHOULD HAVE DONE! BUT NOW IT'S HOPELESS!*—hanging on the wall. A familiar balloony Koons puppy guards the foyer. As Wayne likes to tell his guests, the penthouse was designed by his Parsons-trained interior designer *noona*. His sister has a taste for Italian marble and gold.

In the private dining room atop the spiral staircase, he proudly shows me a refrigerator (Ilsung-made) stocked with special *banchan* made by his grandmother. We order up *chirashi sushi bento* from Genji, the Japanese restaurant in the hotel. We have some *banchan*, quail eggs, and *namool* with it.

"We are the original old-line chaebol family," Wayne says, matter-of-factly, over his *chirashi*. He speaks slowly but smoothly, as if to project an easy mastery over his words.

After we started hanging out at the HBS Café over beers, Wayne would tell me about his grandfather, the legendary Keun Ho Park, who began selling flour and sugar in the 1940s during the Japanese occupation. It's been reported that he was a big-time *chinil-pa*, Japanese collaborator, but Wayne always leaves that part out. The elder Park began trading in a variety of foodstuffs in short supply during the war years. He made his first fortune importing ramen, instant noodles, from Japan. With the profits he bought a couple of textile mills.

Then in the early 1960s, a breakthrough: President Park Chung Hee, under the Second Five-Year Plan, mandated Ilsung to build the first steel mill in the country. He arranged for a hundred-million-dollar loan, at zero interest, by the Korea Industrial Development Bank to Ilsung Steel. Most of the money came from Japanese war reparations. People over the years have charged favoritism, corruption, and worse for this special treatment.

Wayne says simply, "Founder Park was handpicked by President Park for his talent and experience. The steel mill was to be the engine of the country's industrialization drive. And it was. Economy doubled by the seventies."

Company and country seized what history had providentially given them, an urgent, once-in-a-generation opportunity, to grow furiously, not to climb but to leap from the depths of poverty to OECD-level prosperity.

"Today," Wayne says, casually laying down his chopsticks, "our flagship, Ilsung Electron, is the second-largest maker of semiconductors in the world, and the group has interests world-wide in steel, construction, shipbuilding, consumer electronics, and, our newest venture, automobiles."

When I ask him why Ilsung is in so many disparate, unrelated businesses, he looks at me blankly. "Because we *can* be," he says. "Bigger, better."

"But the major industries you're in," I say, "they're highly cyclical. Not to mention capital-intensive. How much does it cost to build a shipyard? And what the hell does shipbuilding have to do with making phones?" I look at him squarely. "Hey, don't you remember all that crap they taught us at the old alma mater? Something called profitability? Cash flow is king?"

"We have to be the biggest group," he says, with a shrug. "We've got three hundred thousand employees, we're in eighty countries, we're bringing in ninety billion a year in revenues. That's twice the size of North Korea's GDP. We're number two today, but we shall be *ichiban* soon. That's our corporate goal." He adds: "Our destiny."

Everyone knows Ilsung owes over thirty billion to the banks, mainly foreign lenders. With the won down, the interest on their loans has skyrocketed. Some analysts have questioned whether Ilsung even has enough cash flow to service the interest payments. But I don't mention any of this. What would be the *humanity* in that? Besides, it's more interesting to believe he has a master plan.

As if reading my thoughts, Wayne says, "That's my inheritance." He looks away. "And my burden."

We seem to be alone in the penthouse. I ask Wayne if the chairman, now in his late sixties, still comes in to work.

"You kidding?" he says. "Old man's in every day by six a.m. I encourage him to retire at lunchtime. Totally ignores me." He shakes his head. "He's downstairs somewhere, taking his power nap."

Wayne is king-in-waiting. He calls himself, only half-jokingly, Prince Charles.

"I suppose Chairman will retire, at some point," he says. "My *dongseng* Yong Suk is certainly counting the days." His younger brother, Kane—another movie-cowboy-name casualty, out of *High Noon*. Though when I first heard his name, I thought it was Cain.

I look at Wayne in the sunlight pouring through the window. He's not as tall as I remember, and his clean, youthful face is offset by wisps of gray hair. He still parts his hair in the middle, in the Japanese male fashion, a leftover from his exchange student days at Waseda University.

Wayne changes topic, preempting any questions about his family. "Can you believe we're going to have a Communist president? Kim Dae Jung wants to bust up chaebol!" he says, incredulous. "We made this country! And the guy didn't even graduate from high school. What's this country come to? Labor unions are dancing in the streets. We might as well be living in Pyongyang. I may emigrate to Japan."

He lets out a sigh. "It's fine, I suppose. As Chairman says, we'll outlast him. One five-year term for president, by constitution; our time horizon is over generations. We always outlast them."

When I asked Jun if he wanted to join me for the lunch at Ilsung, he shook his head. "Chaebol," he said, "they're not like you and me." He told me about the time he attended Kane Park's wedding. Kane was marrying the daughter of then-President Roh. "Big affair, hundreds of guests at the Park country estate," he related. "Catered by Kukje, of course. The guests, we were served *kalbi* and Talbot; the Park family table feasted on filet mignon and Lafite Rothschild. They thought nothing of it. They're entitled to it, because they're royalty." He shook his head, more sadly than angrily. "And you think the wedding was paid for out of their pockets? No way, José. All company expense. They think, Our company, we can do whatever the hell we want. You're just along for the ride.

"But the craziest thing? The *yisei, samsei*, the second and third generations? The talent's been diluted over the generations, not to mention the passion for the family business. Yet they insist on inheriting the mantle and running the show. Everyone knows they're not qualified, but they go through these convoluted, legally dubious succession schemes and become chairmen.

"And the companies? If you have free enterprise, capital should flow out of bad companies and into good companies. Not how it works here." He patted down his cowlick, which sprang right back up. "Worst thing is, these bastards don't recognize they're just members of the Lucky Sperm Club. They think they deserve it. What's that saying? They're born on third base, but they think they hit a triple."

He shook his head. "Look, Koreans aren't pushing for equality. This isn't North Korea, everyone equal. We just want *equal opportunity*. Two things we won't stand for, someone getting out of *koondae* duty and someone getting ahead on something other than merit."

I've read the studies about how the chaebols' entrenched generational-family capital becomes lazy and inefficient. Companies should be dynamic, their capital fluid, flowing out of bad companies and into good companies. I've heard the whispers about the chaebols' systematic corruption, characterized colorfully by some as organized crime racketeering. Everyone knows about the enormous power the big families wield in Korea. The revenues of the top five chaebol groups account for three-quarters of GDP. But their influence extends beyond the market to all reaches of society, economic, political, cultural. They are octopi, their tentacles everywhere.

Wayne tells me about their more subtle power. "You know we chaebol are prohibited from owning financial institutions. A bit silly, since we dominate the deposits and loans at the banks. We're banned from owning media assets, but we might as well be controlling them for all our advertising muscle. No chaebol, no business."

We're interrupted by a man entering the room, no knock. I recognize him from the news, Hyun Chul Kim, *sil-jang* of the all-powerful chairman's office. Recently renamed the Group Strategy & Planning Office ("same shit," according to Jun), the group control tower is known as, simply, "the *Sil*." A call from the *Sil* gets an immediate rise out of the CEOs of the group companies. In his sixties, Kim *Sil-jang* has sharp features, impeccably combed hair, a tight-fitting suit, barely any breathing room. As Koreans say, he looks like he wouldn't bleed if you pricked him with a needle.

Kim seems to have something urgent to convey to Wayne. He looks askance at me.

"It's okay, Ajussi," Wayne says. He uses the familiar Ajussi, a sign the older man is considered part of the family. "He's American."

I remember seeing Kim *Sil-jang* being whisked away to prison, in handcuffs, six, seven years ago. On some charge of misappropriation of company funds or embezzlement or bribery, maybe all of the above. The allegation that stuck was his having procured and managed a corporate slush fund of a trillion won, nearly a billion dollars. Source was fraudulent transfer pricing at overseas subsidiaries; use was, alleged but not proved conclusively, bribes of National Assemblymen and financial regulators. The illicit funds were found parked in hundreds of banking accounts held in the names of group executives.

It was widely understood at the time that Kim was falling on his sword out of loyalty to the chairman. He went to the Big House for a year, had the rest of his sentence suspended, and came out a "made" man. He was named vice chairman and *sil-jang* of the S&PO upon his return. A *caporegime* with his own family to run. Now Clemenza as well as consigliere Tom Hagen. I picture the Ilsung CEOs lining up to kiss the ring on his hand. Within the group, he goes by "Number Two."

While the Prince and Number Two talk in hushed tones, I go sit in front of the TV. Ilsung Display, of course. There's news of more saber-rattling by North Korea. In response to the latest UN sanctions, Secretary-General Kim Jong Il is threatening to launch nuclear-tipped missiles at the US mainland. He vows to "destroy the Yankee devils" in "a sea of fire." What colorful imagery. I can picture the cadres at the Department of Propaganda in the Ministry of Truth getting medals pinned on their chests by the Dear Leader for coming up with this catchy phrase.

Wayne ushers Number Two to the door and then saunters back to the sitting area. He looks over my shoulder at the footage of Dear Leader Kim.

"What a joke," he says. "How's that clown a legitimate ruler? How do his people accept him?" He gets indignant. "His father just passed on the reins to him! What qualifications does he have? What, his son will be ruler after him?"

I search his face for any sign of irony.

"Everything okay?" I ask.

"Another one," he says, with a sigh. When I show no comprehension, he says, "Ajussi got a tip from the General Prosecutor's Office: they're raiding our company headquarters tomorrow. Same crap." By which I assume he means charges of bribery, embezzlement, breach of fiduciary duty.

"Guess we were due," he says, resignedly. "The new administration needs to get it out of its system. Better to get hit with *mae* now and get it over with." Translation: *Time to go to the mattresses.*

I gather that is why the chairman is safely out of sight, purportedly downstairs but nowhere to be found.

"By the way, pardner," Wayne says, lowering his voice. "I may have an assignment for you. Fill you in soon." He's going to make me an offer I can't refuse. "Big deal," he says, his crooked smile a promise of a different kind of adventure.

7

Early January 1998

The lobby lounge at the Koryo Hotel is filled with young couples like us on *sun* meetings. Boy getting introduced to girl, via matchmaker, for possible marriage. Vivaldi's *Four Seasons* comes lightly over the speakers. There is an indoor waterfall at one end of the lounge, the incongruity somehow fitting.

I'm tired, still sleep-deprived, but I'm here on the orders of Minister Choi. My *sun* girl is his niece. She is pretty much as I expected: fair skin, translucent almost, eyes like almonds, slender, of course. Her hair is more brown than black, and, alone among the bride hopefuls here, she has no makeup on.

The minister's wife is here to make the introduction. This is the only daughter of her older sister ("Jee Yeon—just as pretty as her name, no?"). She is a graduate of Ewha and a musician ("as a daughter of any good family should be"). Our matchmaker fingers the constellation of white orbs from Mikimoto dangling from her neck. She makes the obligatory comment about what a fine-looking couple we make ("but, of course, the rest is up to you!").

My parents had an arranged marriage. Umma got married to Abuji after one *sun* meeting. It wasn't uncommon in those days. Umma told us the story, spun over the years into family lore. The summer after her freshman year at Ewha, she was staying at a Buddhist temple, Keumkangsa, in the mountains near Busan. Purifying herself, she said. Every day, morning and evening, she did 108 ceremonial bows to Buddha. Her knees were rubbed raw from the hard wooden floor. But she also secretly did an *inyeon* ritual, praying to Buddha to have her fate revealed and to meet her life's mate.

Abuji's father, my grandfather, attended the same temple. He was taken by the sight of the pretty young woman doing bows day and night. He had never seen such grace in a young person's bows. Halabuji asked the head *bosahl*, bodhisattva, who this devout young woman was, and she vouched for my mother. She told him she was from a good family—parents killed in the 6.25 War but raised by a devoted Buddhist grandmother. "Good family," of course, meant big contributors to the temple.

So the *bosahl*, at Halabuji's behest, arranged the *sun* meeting between my father and my mother. The rest, Umma always said, was fate. Buddha answered her prayers, and the answer was Abuji.

The minister's wife helps us with the orders, me an iced coffee and her niece an orange juice. Her business done, she stands to leave. But before she does, she dispenses one final piece of advice, important, she says: afterward, we need to go get our *koonghap* checked. To see if our stars align, for marital harmony. Good families do not agree to a union without an auspicious *koonghap* rendering, she reminds us. Then she puts her glasses in her Kelly bag and wishes us young people well.

The *sun* girl, I can tell, is waiting for me to say something first. I'm not sure if I'm supposed to speak in the honorific or familiar to her. "What do you play?" I say, opting for half formal–half casual.

"Cello," she says. She speaks so softly I can barely hear her. Her voice is low, much lower than the high pitch that Korean and Japanese women are taught to adopt as a feminine ideal. A pause, then: "You grew up in America."

"*Nep*," I say. "And you in Korea."

She gives a polite partial smile. "Where were you born?"

"Right here," I say. "I mean Seoul, not this exact spot. Or this neighborhood."

"Me, too," she says, charitably.

"We have something in common then." I immediately wish I hadn't emphasized *something*. I drain my glass of iced coffee in one gulp.

"Home is still home, don't you think?"

I nod, a bit too vigorously. "Couldn't agree more."

The man-made waterfall makes more noise than I thought it capable of. It helps with the gaps in our conversation.

"So, how do you see the stock market going?" she says.

"Not sure. Don't really follow the markets."

"Imobu said you work on Wall Street?"

"Can't think of a worse use of my time," I tell her, "than following the daily fluctuations of stock prices or trying to guess this month's unemployment numbers. I'm not interested in information; I'm after wisdom. Not data, but truths."

"You sure you're a banker?" she says, tilting her head.

"Finance is what I do. It's not who I am." I say it a bit more emphatically than I meant to.

"Hmm." She looks right in my eyes. "Okay, I'll bite . . . Who are you then?"

"Ever read Milton in school?" I say. "Any Melville? I've always admired Captain Ahab. I kind of identify with him. Or Satan? Now there's a hero."

She looks hard at me, unblinking.

"Not *Satan* Satan, of course," I clarify. "The character in *Paradise Lost*. You know, 'The mind is its own place, and in itself can make a heaven of hell.' That guy."

Her lips purse, and I detect amusement. Or perhaps just puzzlement. "A banker who reads Romantic novels," she says. "That is, Romantic with a capital R. An MBA who knows his pentameter . . ."

"I'm really a juggler," I say. "I juggle deals. A bond deal, an M&A advisory, another equity offering coming up. That's why I haven't gotten much sleep recently. But really, I can juggle anything. Look." I pick up three sugar cubes and toss them in the air. Two fall through my fingers, rattle across the glass-covered table.

"Impressive," she says, unimpressed. But, I think, not unamused either. "A man of many talents. A *pal-bang me-in.*" A four-character saying I know: an eight-direction beauty, good at many different things. Like uncle, like niece.

The couple at the table next to us is hitting it off. He guffaws, she titters at some witticism, and they're awash in a glow of promise of a future together.

"So you like playing the cello?" I say, turning back to Jee Yeon.

"I am a cellist," she says deliberately, as if to emphasize she, for one, is comfortable with her identity. "I join the Seoul Philharmonic in the spring."

"Ah, Seoul Phils. Good outfit."

She suppresses a smile.

"Okay, I've never really heard of the Seoul Philharmonic. I'm not even sure what cello sounds like. Is it like a big violin?" I hasten to add: "Don't get me wrong. I like music. I listened to a lot of piano growing up."

"Your mother's a pianist? Or your father?"

"My *abuji.* He plays the piano all day long. Used to anyway."

She catches the *used to,* graciously changes course: "Have you had many of these introductions?"

I shake my head, *Anyo.* "You're my first, actually."

She laughs softly, covering her mouth.

"What I mean is, this is my first . . . Not that I expect it to be the first of many . . . Basically, this is probably my last one."

She smiles, though even then it's a half-smile. The other half still a mystery, delicately guarded. I see she has no jewelry on, nothing around her neck, her fingers bare.

"Donated it all," she says, noticing me looking at her hand. "Gave my gold jewelry to the country. Like all good Koreans." She shrugs, as if to punctuate her good civic act with casualness. "The country needed it."

I saw on the news ordinary people waiting in lines for hours to donate their family treasures to support the country in its hour of economic need. Housewives giving their gold wedding bands; old men handing in their gold "luck" keys, a traditional present on the sixtieth birthday. Even kids donating the gold piglet figurines and spoons they received on their *dol*, first birthday. They estimated over a million people participated in the gold-giving campaign. Of course, it barely put a dent in the national debt.

"The Korean 'fighting' spirit."

"You say it like it's a bad thing," she says. She searches for something in her purse. "You've heard of *sam-jong ji-do*?"

Another goddamn four-character saying. Something about a woman's traditional role. "No, but I know *bu-chang bu-su*." Umma used to say the wife follows the husband's song, always with a glint of amusement in her eye.

"A woman's three duties, to father, husband, son." She pulls out a thin cigarette from her purse.

I hesitate a moment before taking her lighter and lighting her cigarette. She holds the cigarette between thin, long fingers. She has a thick callus on the side of her left thumb, I assume from years of cello playing.

"Well, that's not me," she says.

"Okay."

"I have my own plans. I'd like to live abroad. I may want to go to Germany. Berlin has a good symphony."

"Huh." Home isn't just a place to return to; home can be what you want to leave behind.

"Anyway, I want a career. Not as a cellist but as a composer. I don't want kids, at least not for a while." She takes a drag. "I'm not even sure I want to get married."

So, she's an impostor, too. Playing a role, as I am. Acting the dutiful daughter while plotting to escape it all.

"Even if I do get married at some point, I won't take the husband's name. You do know Korean women keep their maiden names, right? I've never understood the Western custom of adopting someone else's name." Her voice has dropped half an octave. "You are who you are."

I look at Jee Yeon more closely. Limpid brown eyes, with a sparkle of what?—independence, defiance maybe. She has a spare, unadorned beauty, a leafless tree in winter. The kind of beauty you find only when you look for it, and even then it reveals itself slowly.

The girl at the adjacent table waves away some smoke, shoots a dirty look our way. Jee Yeon puffs on her cigarette, blows in her direction. Here's more smoke in your heavily mascaraed eye.

Another four-character saying comes to mind: *weh-yoo ne-gang*. Iron hand in velvet glove. I'm swimming in ancient wisdom today.

"So how do we get this *koonghap* test?" I say.

"We go consult a fortune-teller."

"How's it work?"

"They say marital compatibility is determined by your *saju*, the four components of your destiny dictated by the year, month, date, and hour of your birth. Fortune-teller deciphers your nature based on the *saju* and analyzes them according to *ohang*." Seeing my blank face, she says, "You know, wood, fire, earth, metal, and water."

"Right. And you believe in this stuff?"

"That's beside the point," she says, shrugging. "It's Korean custom, centuries old, and it helps achieve harmony in the family." Another puff. "Besides, it's interesting watching these seers fumble around, guessing my character and making things up."

Beethoven's Ninth comes streaming through the lounge speakers, a bit louder. The "Ode to Joy" fills me with amorous courage.

"You make it sound fun. Maybe we can go sometime."

"Maybe. Just make sure you have your birth info. On lunar calendar."

"Korea time or Eastern Standard?"

I think I see a trace of another smile.

Jee Yeon stubs out her cigarette. It takes me a long minute to grasp she's signaling our meeting is over. Just when I was getting the hang of it.

I pull out my StarTAC, and we exchange phone numbers. I tell her, as casually as I can, we should see each other again.

Jee Yeon gives me a half-bow, and I bow back awkwardly.

"By the way?" she says, on her way out. "Captain Ahab is one of my all-time favorite characters. Up there with Heathcliff. Dark heroes are my thing."

The revolving door turns noiselessly in her wake, round and round.

8

Fall 1976

We arrived in America in year of two hundredth birthday of the country. Everywhere red, white, and blue American flags with neat rows of many stars. Americans very proud of their homeland, even though most of them it's not land of their home. From Germany, Ireland, Italy, Mexico, Czechoslovakia, but everybody call themselves American.

Teacher put me as mate with American boy, Ralph Parker. He look like American, blond hair, pink skin, big nose. So nice in American way, smiling to me a lot. I smile back a lot. He ask me if I like baseball. I say yup, and hamburger too.

American Ralph teach me how to read and pronounce hard to say words. Girl, world, and hardest, Laurie. He show me to play American football, different from football I play. Why it's called football when foot not touch ball so much?

Ralph invite me to his house for American meal. His home very big, very old house in a place with gates called Llewellyn Park. Hard to pronounce. Paint on outside falling off, wood floor creak when I step. I hear violin playing always at Parker house, pretty but so sad music. I ask Ralph who is ghost playing violin. He say his dad, Mr. Parker, and he play something called Mendel's Son. Sound like moans in wind. Dinner is pork chops with apple sauce. Parkers drink the milk with dinner. Milk, not water! We sit on wooden bench and eat on old wooden table in kitchen. Big house, but no one dine in dining room.

Ralph's sister called Laurie, not sure older or younger. English strange language, not tell if older or younger sister. No *noona* or *dongseng*. Or older or younger brother. Maybe Americans not care so much about relationships. Laurie has the yellow hair and yellow eyebrow. One day when Ralph not in room, Laurie pull up her shirt and show her small breast at me. Ralph come back in, and she put finger on her lip, so I say nothing. Next time I see her, she smile strange. Our little secret, she tells me. Ralph has older brother, I know older because he has hair on face, he play something called ice hockey. He play with big friends on Parker Pond. They have big shoulders and strange gloves. He is scary *hyung*.

I become Shane to schoolmates. Very American, easy to pronounce. Every time Ralph and I say bye after school, he say "Come back, Shane!" And he laugh, ha ha ha. Ralph introduce me to his friend Michael D'Ario. Michael tell me he's Eye-talian. He look and sound very American to me.

One day he invite Ralph and me to his home for Eye-talian meal. We have spaghetti and meatballs. Mrs. D'Ario keep sprinkling cheese on my spaghetti. It's so stinky, worse than any *dwen-jang* I ever had. But I keep eating and taste not so bad. I think I'm getting American.

In those days, Appa drive us to school in huge red Ford LTD. Appa say, Why come to America to drive small Japanese car?

*

I love American TV. We have nice Zenith color TV. I can stay in front of TV all day. I watch every day Bugs Bunny, *Brady Bunch*—"Marcia, Marcia, MAR-cia!"—and *Gilligan's Island*. I like Marianne with pigtails in hair in beginning. Then I like Ginger, even if she talk funny, like out of breath. I want to be smart like Professor, dress like Thurston Howell the Third. Every night, I wish for them and Gilligan to get off island, but not really.

I like most *I Dream of Jeannie*. Jeannie has powerful blink. She can do anything for her master Major Tony Nelson, like magic, but he not want her to do it. In America, shame to have things done for you. Maybe it goes against what Appa call American can-do spirit. Tony Nelson is very American, he's astronaut (never heard of any astronaut in Korea) and very gentle. Jeannie not American, she from Basenji. But she not speak Basenjian or Farsi, she speak perfect American. She can because she's genie.

Jeannie live in small bottle, but she pop out anytime to serve Master Tony. "Your wish is my command." Jeannie can do simple things with blink. Big things she need to fold her arms in front of her Arab bra and snap her head. Jeannie with her bouncy American breasts, even though like other Americans, she from another place. She also have the golden hair just like American girl. She does not at all look two thousand years old. No way—maybe twenty-five at most. Poor Dr. Bellows, always foiled. *She's done it to me again!* Jeannie too clever for him. She's genie after all.

Sad day in my life when Jeannie marry Master Tony. Why she did it? Her family back in Basenji against, and I'm against. Does she really, gulp, love him? Or she had to because ancient rule to serve lifetime the man (what if girl?) who release her from bottle? Maybe not her free will. Maybe a genie's destiny. But this is America, land of freedom! Still, Major Roger Healey feel hurt and jealous like me. I can understand Major Roger. Who not want magical American Jeannie? In my country, we have ghosts. In America, they have genies.

One night I dream of Jeannie. I rub bottle and she come out with hiss and smoke and say I am master and my wish her command. I tell her that's OK, I don't want to be master. Jeannie's hair turn brown, she look like her evil twin sister Jeannie, and she say, Then *I* will be your master. Then evil Jeannie pull me hard and kiss me, her tongue go down my throat, all the way down there. I feel her tongue on my thingy, I tell her stop. But she not stop, her tongue wrapped around my thingy like snake and squeezing. She say, *Your wish, your wish.* Her American breasts pop out of her Arab bra and bounce, up and down, *boing boing*. She lift me up with her in NASA rocket, up up up, I feel pressure up against my face. We reach top, then we plunge down, spiral into ocean. When I wake up, I feel strange and my underpants and sheet all wet and Elmer's Gluey. This is first time I have dream in American.

9

Mid-January 1998

Faces blur and voices become a dull roar, and I have to focus to orient myself. Back in the United States; New York, midtown Manhattan, Citywide Bank office, Thames conference room. Wood-paneled walls, the conference table dark and luminous as the sea on a clear night. I haven't slept in seventy-two hours.

Director Suh's visage comes into view, along with the rest of the Mop PTFT, jet lag melting their faces as in a Salvador Dalí painting. They're surrounded by a horde of lawyers and bankers, all in dark suits. I imagine these professionals getting ready for work in the morning, putting on their suits and ties. Each of them, like generations of serious working men before them, tying a noose around his neck to go to work. Choking himself to a slow death.

From the noise around the table I make out something about "the Rock" and a "change offer." ROK, Republic of Korea. It comes to me, in fragments. A meeting to hammer out the terms of the debt exchange offer. Banks from around the world involved in the exchange, over two hundred of them, represented by the dozen lead creditors in this room. You can tell the commercial bankers from the investment bankers. Commercial bankers are the ones in earnest Paul Stuart suits and Rolexes, Piguets. Investment bankers wear Huntsman suits; bespoke, not custom-tailored, Charvet shirts (French cuff, *bien sûr*); Hermès ties; and, to show they're above conspicuous consumption, plastic Timex Ironman watches. It doesn't matter, a noose is a noose. I feel mine pulling tighter.

The bankers are balking at taking a "haircut," a discount on the face value, on the debt. One of them with a raspy voice can be heard over the others.

"Why should America Bank get penalized?" he says, finger poking the air. "We at America Bank a) rolled over our credit to stop the bleeding, b) extended the rollover by another month, and c) are now stuck holding degraded Rock paper." Both kinds of banker like to talk in bullet points, not complete sentences.

"The lenders in this room," another banker says, in dulcet tones, "from here and the UK and Germany, have been generous in extending liquidity to the Rock." Everyone knows the banks were forced into their rollover, arms twisted by the New York Fed and the Bundesbank, for fear of a systemic global credit meltdown.

"We did it because we have faith in the Rock government to do the right thing," he adds helpfully.

The usual bad cop/good cop routine, acted out for the benefit of the Korean officials.

Director Suh sits impassive, arms crossed, lips curled down at the ends. After nearly every meeting with bankers, he tells me, "Americans talk too much." To him, all Westerners are Americans.

I sit in a back row, along with Jack and the other "minions," as the Monkey likes to call us. The integrity of my sleep cycle has been compromised, and I can barely keep my eyes open, much less follow the discussion. Two all-nighters and then thirteen hours gained somehow in the air between Seoul and JFK. Einstein was right: time is a tricky little bugger. I close my eyes and hold my breath, nearly succeed in blacking out.

I'm jolted awake by the familiar sound of Tom Brogan's gruff voice from the front of the room. He's one of the few investment bankers allowed in these proceedings; he's one of their own. Jack is sure Brogan is one of "the Kappa Beta Phi secret hand-shaking mofos." The Grand Ass-Wipe, for all we know.

"Gentlemen, do you know what we're looking at?" Brogan says, in the direction of the Korean officials.

The Koreans look blankly at one another.

"I'll tell y'all what we're looking at," he says. "We're looking into the abyss. The Rock has fifteen billion in debt to international banks coming due in the next two weeks. Your sovereign debt has been downgraded by Moody's and S&P. You're down to two-point-five billion in FX reserves." He pauses, for effect. "If we don't get this debt exchange done—right goddamn now—there is no rescue program. Your fine country is going into default. A.k.a. the shitter."

Every deal has its own language. Figuring out the ever-changing grammar is the key. Linguistic fluency is a necessary but not a sufficient condition. Going into the shitter is pretty well near universal language.

Gandalf of Sterling, who's been sitting quietly, is not to be upstaged. "And you banks," he says, standing up. "Let's face it. All of you made a bad credit decision. You need to suck it up and accept the penalty."

"What kind of a haircut we talking?" a banker asks.

"Who determines the pricing?" another says.

"—critical to have price discovery—"

"—just get the Rock government to guarantee our debt—"

"—no, the market has to decide—"

"—try a Dutch auction—"

"We cannot," Suh says, evenly. "Our new president will not accept open pricing."

A pall of quiet falls over the room.

Finally, William Path, the self-proclaimed éminence grise of Citywide Bank, stands up. He has sparse white hair with a sharp part, and he wears a yellow bow tie. "Gentlemen, gentlemen," he says, the voice of reason. "The Rock government will not get an open pricing mechanism past its parliament. We need a *negotiated* solution."

The word *negotiated* is the sound of a chime in the woods, clear, ringing.

"What kind of pricing we talking about here?" someone asks timidly.

"Say, two-twenty-five bips over LIBOR for the one-year loans," Path offers. "Two-fifty over on the two-years." There's some grumbling around the table. "Really the only way to get this done in the time frame required," he says, ever the statesman. "Then we can move on to the bond offering, get eight to ten billion in new capital in the Rock's coffers."

They go back and forth on what they start calling the Thames Plan.

"Even if we agree to this Thames Plan, the banks here own only 35 percent of the debt," someone points out. "How do we get the other hundred-eighty-seven lenders to sign on?"

"The abyss!" Brogan reminds everyone.

Several people start talking at once. The voices in the room overlap, grow louder, English mixed with German-inflected English and bad Japanese English, a Tower of Banking Babble.

Umma once told me an old folktale about a newlywed couple living in the countryside. The husband had to go to town for some business, and the bride asked him to buy her a woman's comb. Knowing how absentminded he could be, she pointed up to the moon, a thin crescent of light in the sky, and told him, if he forgot, just look up at the moon, and he'd be reminded of the shape of her comb.

Several days later, after finishing up his business in town, the husband remembered he had to get something for his wife. Recalling something about the moon, he looked up and saw a full moon lighting up the sky. He went to the nearest shop and asked the shopkeeper, "Do you have something for my wife that looks like the moon up there?" The shopkeeper saw the round moon, and he said, "I have just the thing." He brought out a silver hand mirror. "The new thing for young women," he said. "You look into it, and you can see yourself, so you can get prettied up."

Happy with his gift, the man returned to his village and gave his wife the hand mirror. She looked into the smooth glass, and what did she see there but a pretty, young woman! "What's the meaning of this?" she cried out. "Why have you brought another woman back from town?" She ran out into the yard and, breaking down in tears, said to her housekeeper, "I asked for a comb, and he brought back a strange woman." The elderly housekeeper said, "Let me see, ma'am," and took the mirror. What she saw was the face of a wrinkled old woman. "Why, it's just an old woman." The mistress took the mirror back and showed the image to the housekeeper. "See, it's a young woman," she cried.

While the two women went back and forth, a boy came by, chewing on a stick of taffy. He was curious, so he took the mirror and peered into it. There was a boy eating his taffy. "Hey, give me back my *yut*," he yelled. "It's mine!" He raised his arm to strike the boy, and the boy also raised his arm, ready to fight. The boy started crying loudly. Just then, the village elder came by to see what the fuss was about. "Let me see that," he said, taking the unfamiliar round object. "Why, it's a grandfather," he said, heatedly. "You should be ashamed at your age to be meddling in a fight between boys."

As the old man angrily shook the hand mirror, it slipped from his grasp and dropped to the ground. The glass shattered into a hundred pieces. The old man, the boy, and the two women all fell silent and stared at the broken glass at their feet.

I look around the conference room, and the faces are jagged reflections on a hundred shards of glass. They have idiot grins, lupine eyes; they look dark, disjointed, desperate.

A whiff of cigarette comes from the back of the room, and I recognize it, Marlboro. I breathe it in, then hold it, try to recapture the smell.

I wonder if you can retrieve what is lost. Abuji, his Marlboro smell. Umma singing her plaintive folk songs at the kitchen sink. Our old house in Seoul, with its dirt front yard, where I used to play *ttakji*. The pinwheel on the handlebar of my bicycle spinning bright colors in the breeze. What if we had stayed?

I hold my breath in, just a bit longer. Can you have a memory of what might have been?

The voices flicker, and I feel myself getting smaller, fading into the past.

10

I gotta tell ya, I love my New York Yankees. Their nickname stands for Americans where I'm from, but here they belong to New York. The Bronx Bombers, sometimes called the Bronx Zoo Animals. Their cool pinstripe uniforms, the *N* over *Y* logo, the Yankee Stadium cheer, "Let's go Yan-kees, bum-bum-bada-dum." Billy Martin, Catfish Hunter, Reggie Jackson—*Reg-gie! Reg-gie!*—and my favorite, Thurman Munson. Big, bad Bombers, with their bushy mustaches, they're the American cool.

Thurman is captain of the team, but Reggie says he's the straw in milkshake, because he's the slugger and he likes to stir things. America is the land of sluggers, and Reggie is the biggest slugger of them all. Well, maybe greatest after Babe Ruth, a really fat slugger from a long time ago named after a chocolate bar. Thurman had a fight with Reggie, and Reggie had a fight with the manager Billy. Punching your manager! It could never happen in Korea, never ever. Only in America. Land where big, mustached sluggers can beat up who they want, even their teachers.

Those Yanks are always fighting, but doesn't matter, because they're awesome anyway. We kick the butts of the hateful Boston Red Sox. Red Sox suck. We'll lose to them when pigs will fly. Boy, I really hate that Carlton Fisk. He had fight with Captain Thurman too. Yankee fans cheer when players fight. With Thurman and Reggie and Sparky, with bubble gum in his right cheek, we'll go the whole way this season. We'll win World Series, and we'll be champions of the world! Not just of America but the whole world!

They keep talking about the Son of Sam in the TV news. It makes me think of a famous book by Dr. Seuss I read. Son of Sam, Sam I am. They say he's disturbed and did really terrible things. They tried and tried to catch him. When they finally did, they put him in the jail, for a long time. Poor guy. I think of him in jail going, *I will not eat green eggs and ham. I do not like them, Sam I am.* He should know sometimes no matter how bad it is, you just gotta close your eyes and eat it. Just like Umma says.

I get my own room this summer. Away from my *dongseng* finally. Independence day! I put up my first poster on bedroom wall, Farrah Fawcett in sexy red swimsuit. You can see through her swimsuit! No such thing as sexy in my old country. Farrah has blonde, wavy hair, not like Korean girls' straight hair. And those white teeth, like my favorite gum Chiclets. Yeah, she's the American fox.

New York City is just across a dirty river from where we live. They call it the Big Apple, I don't know why. Nobody explains things to newcomers in America. So much I don't know but am curious about. I get "sunny-side up" on eggs, but what is "over easy"? Nowhere to find the answer, not even in a dictionary. Anyway, Big Apple is where the action lives. In *Encyclopedia Americana*, it says New York City is the money, media, and art capital of the world. It is also home of my Yankees, though it's also where Son of Sam lives. Maybe you gotta have bad with the good. I've made up my mind I'm gonna live in Big Apple when I grow up. Sure better than Fort Lee.

Last month they had a blackout in NYC. Didn't know America, land of plenty, could run out of electricity, but they did. TV showed scenes of many unhappy people and big fires. Learned a new word, "looting." Sounds like shooting, and hooting. Looting people carry TV sets out of stores, break windows. Black people throw things at white policemen. First time I see angry American people. News guys keep talking about race. They say it's a big cause of the riots. Appa shakes his head. "Black, brown, white," he says, "they're all Americans. Don't they know how good they have it?"

Guess there's anger in America, too. Not all sunshine and happy here. Lot of yelling and fighting. And looting. Maybe not so different after all.

11

Late January 1998

A curl of smoke hangs over the microphone, rolling in the red and blue and yellow lights. "My Way" is crooned as it can only be by Asian businessmen at karaoke, lyrics mangled, refrains overly expanded: "I did it . . . MYYYYY waaaayyyyyy . . ."

To my left someone with a familiar face is passed out, his torso lying perpendicular to his upright legs. On the table in front of me, a couple is entwined in a slow dance, trying mightily to keep their balance. They are the Mop PTFT members I've spent the last month with, but the serious, pinched masks they wear during the day are replaced by the goofy faces of the blissfully inebriated, abetted by the club *agassi*.

They pass round after round of *poktanju*, "bomb shots," and insist I keep up. "All for one," they toast, in unison. My face feels flushed, and I feel a heaviness coming over me, but I announce my fineness, protest repeatedly for all to hear, "Really, I'm fine."

I ponder the enormous confluence of events that brought me here, to this *room salon* in the basement of a building in Gangnam, at this propitious point in the history of human civilization. Isn't it remarkable, through the shiny miracle of chance that touches the universe, that I was born in Korea in the mid-1960s, that Korea achieved miraculous prosperity through the seventies, under the iron hand of a sunglasses-wearing dictator, that it then, at the cusp of a new millennium, blew it all by leveraging itself to the hilt with foreign debt? That the government got a bailout package from the IMF and brought Phipps and me in on a mission impossible? Cue music—*dan dan dan dan dan da dan dan da da da*—*Your mission, should you choose to accept it, is to rescue the homeland from complete and utter ruin. Good luck, Shane. This tape will self-destruct in five seconds . . .* Nothing short of extraordinary, the series of happy accidents that allowed us to execute an exchange of bank loans for government-guaranteed bonds, the initial but critical gate in the ROK rescue program, that prompted the Mop officials to want to show us their appreciation for a job well done over drinks, in proper Korean style, in a hostess bar, drinking, singing, and, as everyone keeps saying, *bonding*.

"Young Lee *Yisa*," Director Suh says to me. "Round one done. Now just the bond offering to get new capital in. No problem, right?"

"No problem, sir," I say, with as much confidence as I can muster.

"Fighting!" he shouts, raising a clenched fist as an exclamation point. "So, how you like Mirage? This *agassi*, your 'partner,' is investment-grade?"

He guffaws, doesn't wait for a response. "Here, you drink cyclone *poktanju*," he says, giving the beer glass a deft spin of the wrist, inducing a swirl. He holds up his index finger: "One shot."

The director watches intently as I try to chug it, spilling half on my shirt, return the glass to him. He chortles, slaps me on the back.

Suh then takes off his shoe and pours beer and whiskey into it. His colleagues watch, amused, the *agassi*, impressed. He hands the alcohol-sloshing shoe to a *kwajang*, orders, "One shot!" The subordinate takes the shoe gratefully, with two hands, and takes a large gulp. He says "*Weeha-yuh!*," passes around the leaking brogue.

You have to hand it to Korean men. Where else can middle-aged farts with quotidian day jobs become kings at night? Where aspiration morphs into reality, even if just for an evening. Young, nubile hostesses pour drinks for them, feed them pieces of fruit, call them Oppa (never Ajussi!) and tell them how *virile* they are. And what's with these rooms behind closed doors? You wonder what lurid dramas are unfolding behind all the other doors in this establishment. Maybe a businessman drowning his marital sorrows in scotch and song. Or perhaps a lovers' quarrel between a jaded hostess and a customer who thought it was about a romance. Secrets being shared, promises made. Narratives of desire and jealousy, disappointment and redemption. Maybe that's what life is, a sum of people I'll never meet but I know, of private dramas I'll never see but am familiar with.

"'Sup, little buddy!" Jack says, putting his arm over my shoulder. I don't know what I'm annoyed by more, his unconscious equating of me with Gilligan or the oh-too-easy dropping of his arm over my shoulder in that casual domineering way tall people have.

Jack pulls me closer, says, "Hey, DJ, how come your women so fine? And the men . . . I mean, you Korean guys are short, skinny, kind of . . . feminine." Jack is six foot three, making him easily the tallest person in any setting in Korea. He was captain of the Princeton lacrosse team, a fact he manages to mention at every opportunity, and he has a born athlete's easy way with women. "No offense—"

The Mop *kwajang* thrusts two shot glasses in his face, and Jack says, "What, just a boilermaker."

Then the official takes a lighter and lights the glasses on fire, saying, "Firebombs!" Two flames of blue-yellow shoot up, dance in the dark. He drinks one and offers the other to Jack.

"Whoa," Jack says, eyes widening.

"Investment banker," says the *agassi* seated between us. "You guys, like, play with stocks and M&A and insider trading and all that stuff, right?"

All that stuff, I nod.

Jack is running his fingers though his partner's long, straight hair. The Jack I know is a banker with a soul. His interests go beyond Wall Street; he'll be the first to tell you his curiosity about

Asian cultures dates back to his days as an East Asian Studies major at Princeton. He's also a victim of the Western mythologizing of Asian feminine beauty. He starts singing, a cappella, "Oh, me so horny . . . me love you long time."

His partner giggles, hand over her mouth.

Jack says, winking at me, "She wants me bad."

She turns to me, asks me to translate to him: Does he have chest hair?

When Jack tears his shirt open, popping a button, to show his chest hair, the *agassi* around the table have a collective giggle fit. They call him "hairy, big-nosed barbarian" and "AIDS carrier." I don't translate. One girl pulls at some chest hair, thinks it's the funniest thing in the world.

"Wonderful Tonight" blasts through the trash compactor-sized speakers on either side of our couch.

"Can you smell it, kid?" Jack says, too loudly, pushing his face into mine.

"Sweat and beer?" I say. "Cheap perfume?"

"Possibility. The night is filled with fucking possibility." He gives me a fist bump.

They call me to the stage. I protest I don't know any songs, but they'll have none of it. I can't think of any cheesy oldies befitting this environment, so I cue up Radiohead. "I'm a creep, I'm a weirdooooo . . ." I sing, a bit off but, I'm convinced, with feeling. The guitarist tries his best to keep up. *"What the hell am I doing here . . . I don't belong here . . ."* I wail. *"She run, run, run, run, run . . . RUUUUNNNNN."*

I sit down to a stunned hush, then a smattering of polite applause. An *agassi* asks, "Oppa, what mean 'creep'?"

"Um, *jjoda*," I say.

She laughs, says I must be a *kanchup* from the North. Only North Korean spies would use that corny old expression.

I notice her eyes are perfect coins. I look around the table—all the girls are pretty but in an eerily similar way. They have the same round eyes, the size of quarters, aquiline noses, white skin, incongruously bulbous breasts. They look . . . Western.

"The power of cosmetic surgery," Jun bellows. "A society that values beauty," he continues, in a lower voice. "Even if medically enhanced. Hence the double-eyelid surgery, the breast implants— saline, not the fake-looking silicone stuff. Seoul has become the cosmetic surgery capital of the world."

"Just not natural," I say.

"So what," Jack shouts. "Better than not being good to look at."

"They all go to the same cosmetic surgeons on Dongho-ro," Jun says. "Beauty Alley, they call it. The madam here gets them a group discount."

My partner looks different from the others. She has short black hair and porcelain white skin. She has the regulation round eyes, but a hairline scar at the side of her mouth gives her a delicately damaged air. I ask her for her name, and she says, speaking in the honorific, "Yun Hwa *yeyo*." She keeps her head bowed a touch, doesn't look at me.

Another man takes the stage, singing "It's Now or Never," unironically, and I can barely hear her.

"Pretty name," I blurt.

"Not my real name," she says, close to my ear.

I ask what her real name is, and she just smiles, faintly. Her lips form a red bow.

"I like Radiohead." Of course she does.

While everyone is turned to the man onstage, I see her look the other way, her eyes cast down. What I thought was serenity in her face is, more, sadness.

"So, seeing anybody?" I say. "Outside of work, I mean."

"Love is a luxury in our line of work." She downs her shot. "Can't afford it."

"Okay."

"It's not sex we sell, you know," she says. "It's romance, or the illusion of romance. There's a difference."

"But you sell."

"Don't we all sell? Something or other?"

Maybe she has a point. Except I don't know if I'm a seller or buyer.

"Look at those two," an *agassi* yells from across the table. "Ask her for her number."

"Get a fucking room," Jack says, guffawing. He cracks himself up.

I feel a dizziness coming on. It may be the lack of sleep or the liquor catching up to me. I hold my breath, try to clear my head. Three and a half minutes on my watch this time. The old lungs aren't letting me down.

I open my eyes to see Yun Hwa casually brushing away a Mop guy's hand grazing her thigh.

I excuse myself to go to the bathroom, a tiny stall at the far end of the room. Closing the door, I bring my face close to the mirror, then pull away, then close again. I study objectively the face staring back at me. There's a mop of unruly, ink-black hair surrounding a blotchy red face, the telltale Asian drinking affliction, bloodshot eyes. A smile sloppy but genuine. Stretch the smile, count the teeth. My, what big teeth you have. Is that joy I detect? From hopefulness, from *homefulness*? From a connection made with a pretty stranger, Yun Hwa, or whatever her real name is? Or is it Jee Yeon I'm thinking of? Who knows, maybe Jee Yeon is my soul mate. Why not? From a new sense of belonging? These are my band of brothers. Brethren in arms— *we few, we happy few*—shedding sweat and blood together. Is this what home feels like?

I'm overcome by an urge to call Jee Yeon. Some unfinished business there, methinks.

"Surprised?" I say, trying my damnedest not to slur my words, which seem to echo off the bathroom walls.

Jee Yeon doesn't seem surprised. I get the sense that's the way she is, unperturbed, rarely surprised. "It's late, isn't it?" she says, quietly.

"Not too," I say, covering my other ear to hear better.

"You've been drinking, I see."

"Not so much," I say, suppressing a burp.

"Turning Korean already."

Lighthearted banter! I've got her right where I want her. "So, I've been thinking . . . ," I say and lose my train of thought.

She waits, then laughs softly. She kindly helps me out. "My orchestra is giving a preview performance at the Seoul Performing Arts Center in two weeks . . . if you'd like to come." And, she adds, if I don't mind sitting with her family.

"I don't," I say. "I mean, sure, why not? Love to come. Nothing I'd rather do." And I'm surprised at how much I mean it.

I want to tell her about my evening, my newfound brethren, maybe share some of my dreams with her, the good ones anyway. And hear about her life, and her dreams. But she says, "Good night then, Dae Joon-*ssi*." She has a knack for leaving me hanging, wanting more. Still, the sound of my name rolling off her tongue leaves me with a goofy grin.

By the time I come out of the bathroom, the party's over and people are getting up. Only Jack remains seated, demanding some satisfaction from his partner.

"Coming with, right?" Jack says to her, as she gets up to leave. "Right??"

The men give one another big brotherly hugs. "Brothers in arms!" we shout, in English. *Beu-rah-duh!* The *agassi* bow, wish us a safe ride home.

Yun Hwa and I shake hands, and I say I'll see her soon. She whispers, *Soon.* I search her eyes, and she gives a slight nod.

At the exit, we see Jack's partner saying goodbye to another customer, hugging him, saying, in her breathy way, "Call me, Oppa."

"Traitorous bitch," Jack says, slurring. He seems more befuddled than indignant.

We spill out onto the street. The air is bracing, fresh and cold. A light snow begins to fall.

"May the bridges we burn . . . light the way!" Jack shouts, spreading wide his arms. Snow falls on his upturned face and around him on the sidewalk. He struggles to keep his balance.

I hail a taxi, the black kind for foreigners.

"Where to, buddy?" Jack says, his eyes closing.

"Home." I fold his large frame into the back seat. "Off you go." I tell the driver the hotel name and close the door over Jack's protest, give it two taps to get going.

I start heading back to Mirage when I see Yun Hwa coming out of the entrance. Puffs of white float in the air, land gently on her head and shoulders, and she shivers.

Seeing me approach, she says, "I could use another drink."

"Sure, why not," I say.

As we get into a white taxi, there's an old man on the street, his back bent at a forty-five-degree angle. He crooks a bony finger at me, says, "You don't fool me."

"*Neh*?" I say.

"You don't fool me for a second," he says, before turning away and stumbling into the cold night.

*

The place Yun Hwa takes us to is a *pojang macha*, a late-night street eatery. We step inside the vinyl tent, and the smoke and heat from a burning fire unexpectedly kindle an atavistic impulse in me, for hearth and home. The food being grilled and fried and boiled feels like a warm welcome home.

Yun Hwa chooses for us a bench in front of the food counter. She has erased most of her makeup, and she wears large black glasses.

"Blind as an owl," she explains. But the glasses can't hide her forlorn beauty. A face that could launch a thousand ballistic missiles.

She orders two bottles of Jinro soju. I order *ttukbokki* and *odeng*. Dishes from my childhood. Steam rises in tendrils from the *odeng* broth. The first sip of the broth rings a bell on a long-forgotten door.

She pours some soju in my glass, before catching herself. "Force of professional habit," she says.

I take the bottle, pour for her instead.

"I know you probably judge," she says, downing her drink.

"Have wondered why. Why your line of work."

I know all about the long tradition of *giseng*, dating back to the Koryŏ Dynasty. They were artists, entertainers sanctioned by the court, trained for years in poetry and song to entertain the royalty and *yangban*. Some were courtesans, too, but they played a legitimate role in traditional society. But Yun Hwa hardly looks or acts like a courtesan.

She shrugs her shoulders. "Rich guys come to get served by us," she says. "And we serve them." She takes a gulp. "People think they come to get drunk, abuse us, do obscene things. But mostly the guys come not to commit sins but to confess them. To us. Ends up more a confessional."

"That'd make you . . . a priestess?"

She just drinks her soju. "I accept my life as is. Don't expect someone like you to understand."

"Fair enough. But what if one of these guys gets, uh, aggressive with you?"

"You know about *eunjang-do*?" she says. "In the Chŏsun days, young women would carry around a small silver knife inside their sleeves. It was to protect themselves from unwanted advances from a man, to preserve their honor."

"Huh?" The soju is fogging my brain.

"If they were about to be sullied, couldn't avoid it, they'd use it to commit suicide."

"Why kill yourself? Why not just use it on the attacker?"

She lets out a sigh. "Well, I carry an *eunjang-do*." She drinks.

I can't tell if she's being figurative.

The *ajumma* behind the counter places another heaping bowl of *odeng* broth in front of us, and Yun Hwa says, "We'll eat it well, Imo." She tells me the woman operates this place all night. She's putting her son through *hagwon*, cram school, so he may have a shot at getting into a "Sky" university. Sacrificing so he may have an opportunity for a better life.

"Sky?" I say.

"You know, Seoul National, Korea, Yonsei?" she says. "The SKY schools. What they all reach for."

"Ah, like HYPSM. You know, Harvard, Yale—"

"This little guy," she says, holding up the green soju bottle. "Can't get to sleep without him." She smiles, a bit wistfully.

Yun Hwa's sadness arouses something primal in me, an urge to protect. But I also know it's an urge I need to stifle. She's a spirit in the night, I tell myself. Materialized here so we may lift a little of the sadness off each other, just for tonight.

"The road to alcoholism is paved with bottles of soju," I offer. Probably not the right thing to say.

She pretends not to hear me. "Isn't it nice here? Like a cocoon." Or a womb, I think. She turns to me. "Oppa, we can just stay here all night, and drink." She clinks her glass against mine.

"We could . . ." I feel myself descending to a dark, familiar place.

The *pojang macha* has nearly emptied. We're the last customers remaining. I look at my watch: it's four a.m. "I do have an early morning—"

Yun Hwa sighs, finishes her bottle in one gulp. She has some difficulty pushing herself off from the table, and I grab her elbow to support her.

Outside, the streets are covered in a sheet of fresh snow. As we walk, I say, "Something beautiful about walking in snow no one's walked on. Don't you think?"

She nods in agreement.

"Brings me back to childhood . . ."

Staring straight ahead, she says, "Is your life going the way you thought it'd go?"

The question stumps me. Stops me right in my soju-addled tracks.

I start to say something about just following my destiny.

"Aren't we all condemned to our destinies?" she says.

I stand there, and she turns to me. She slides her arms under mine, plants her head on my shoulder. The snow whirls down softly, silently all around us.

Yun Hwa's words ring in my head as I put her in a taxi. She rolls down the window and looks at me, gives me a sad smile. I wave goodbye until she's gone.

*

In the morning, I come in late to work, feeling a bit like an impostor for my performance last night. But no one says a word. I learn the first rule of drinking in Korea: everything that happens in a room salon stays in that room. Only one colleague, a woman VP in the Seoul office, comments, in passing, "You survived."

The Monkey tells me I look like shit.

Jack arrives an hour after I do, in worse shape. He mumbles an excuse about an important early call with New York.

In the meeting room, we're already gathered, ready to go over a slide presentation for the bond roadshow. The first slide is projected onto a wall: "Top 5 Reasons Jack Did Not Answer the Bell This AM." Jack looks confused.

"Reason number five," the Monkey reads. "Had an important conference call with NY in a.m. no one knew about.

"Number four. Hotel operator put in EST for the wake-up call.

"Three. Had a hard time getting a cab.

"Two. Got in some extra sets on the bench in morning workout.

"And the number one reason Jack did not answer the morning bell . . . He got shit-faced the night before." Thunderous applause and whooping all around.

Jack holds his arms up, executes an exaggerated bow. "Glad to be a source of amusement for you," he says, good-naturedly. "Fuck you very much."

We're told the second rule of drinking, known as "ATFBB": *Answer the effing bell, bitch.* The *kunbeis,* the singing, the fraternal hugs feel distant, happenings in a faraway land. Yun Hwa's face comes back to me, but it seems disembodied, a character in a long-forgotten book. And the connection, if there was one, lost.

The Monkey comes by our desks. "Everything copacetic?" he says. Never a salutary lead-in from a guy who has a sign on his desk reading, I'LL BE NICER IF YOU'LL BE FUCKING SMARTER. He picks up the draft credit memo Jack and I have been working on. "The credit stats are the stats," he mumbles, flipping pages. "But, remember, it's about the narrative. You gotta use the numbers to tell a story. We are *storytellers.* Use your imagination to sell . . ." He stops reading, wrinkles his nose. He drops the pages in a heap from splayed fingers, as if he's touched dog shit.

"Better put your thinking caps on, gentlemen," the Monkey says. "Sharpen your pencils. Two weeks to bond launch." He reminds us, unnecessarily, "*D minus thirty.*" One month to bond pricing day.

II

He who learns must suffer
And even in our sleep, pain that cannot forget
Falls drop by drop upon the heart,
And in our despair, against our will,
Comes wisdom to us by the awful grace of God.

Aeschylus, *Agamemnon*

II

12

Late January 1998

As the meeting starts, I think of the Zen koan about the sound of one hand clapping.

We're having a final planning session for the sovereign bond offering, and we have the client to ourselves. The Sterling team is boycotting the meeting after a pissing contest over whose logo should appear on the bottom left, the lead position, of the investor presentation. Phipps argued alphabetical; Sterling insisted on the reverse, since it is alphabetical on the prospectus, the official selling document. I did not endear myself to the Monkey when I suggested maybe leaving out the logos altogether; after all, isn't it the Korean government's roadshow? Gandalf of Sterling decided to take a stand, "on principle," he said with a huff, and declared a boycott.

So this morning, after weeks of Catoesque table-pounding with "*Sterlingo delenda est!*" the Monkey has the stage to himself. Just the Mop team and him, in a one-handed meeting. And he is *wired.* He goes over a slide comparing Korea's credit statistics with those of OECD member countries and the other Asian Tigers. "Here's Taiwan, Hong Kong, Singapore, Korea . . . last," he says. "But, *but*: pro forma for the rollover and eight to ten billion in new capital, we jump to second place!"

In his exuberance, the Monkey makes suggestion after suggestion on the presentation. Jack, Jun, and I had spent day after day drafting and revising and polishing the presentation, now "v68," to be used in the all-important meetings with bond investors. "We need more bullet points," the Monkey says. "Can we do these slides . . . in portrait?"

"The *fuuuuck*," Jack says through clamped teeth. "We have to redo every goddamn page. This is payback—it's got to be."

Late last night the Monkey had called the PTFT office at the Mop, and Jack picked up. The Monkey demanded someone fax him a memo he left there. Jack, running on fumes and in no mood to play errand boy, said he was busy, could it wait till morning? At which the Monkey exploded, saying, "Do you know who the fuck I am?" I could hear his voice clear through the phone.

Jack said, calmly, "Do you know who the fuck *I* am?"

"You?" the Monkey shouted. "How the fuck should I know who you are, you pissant!"

"Good," Jack said, and hung up.

Jack has been keeping his distance from the Monkey this morning.

"Can it get any better than this?" the Monkey says. "There's a poetry, *music*, to doing a deal right. A form of excellence. When it's done just right, a deal transcends human endeavor. It's godlike." He's no longer the Monkey; he's a pig, blissfully wallowing in shit.

"Oh, joy," Jack says.

To the Monkey and Jack and all the other bankers, this bond offering is a trophy transaction, but still just a deal. For me, it represents the last good chance to save Korea from financial doom. We have to market it exactly right to generate robust investor demand. Then there's the pricing of the bonds—a delicate zero-sum game between the issuer and the investors. Bad pricing could bring down the government and even ruin the country. Where do my loyalties lie: my company or my home country? I can see the thin layer of ice melting off the branches out the window. I keep my eyes on an icicle resembling a hanging sword—a sword of Damocles, in my mind—melting, from top to bottom, a drop at a time. There's a rhythm to the dripping. I feel a dizziness coming on.

Director Suh has his eyes closed, meditating or dozing off, I can never tell for sure.

I overhear a conversation from the back of the room. A Mop *team-jang* and one of his underlings:

Team-jang: Ahem, how's the team doing?

Junior colleague: *Neh, Team-jangnim*, the team's doing fine, working hard.

Team-jang: (. . .)

Junior: (. . . ?) Uh, shall I get them together tonight? It's been a while since we had a team *dinner*.

Team-jang: Perhaps. But if they have plans . . .

Junior: I'm sure they don't. You haven't had a drink with us for a while.

Team-jang: It has been a while . . .

Junior: I beg you to consider. It's necessary for the team's morale.

Team-jang: Shall we then?

Junior: I'll make the arrangements.

Team-jang: (. . .)

Junior: (???)

Team-jang: Perhaps our foreign adviser guests also available?

Junior: I'm sure they'd appreciate the opportunity to join . . . and pay.

Team-jang: Leave it to you.

Junior: *Neh, Team-jangnim*, I'll get them right away.

The junior guy gets up to go look for Jun.

News comes over the TV of the annual ROK-US joint military exercise, called Operation Foal-Eagle, being conducted near Incheon. File videos of B-2 bombers and F-52 fighter jets swishing overhead, big cannons that fire like pistons, forbidding aircraft carriers looming on the horizon. Parachutes pop open in the sky, small flowers blooming, and Korean and American troops land side by side on a beach.

North Korea has responded with a military parade. There's footage of hundreds of neat columns of soldiers goose-stepping across People's Square, with a precision the envy of the Rock-ettes. Koreans, North and South, do synchronization like nobody else. The Dear Leader watches the march with a beneficent smile, blesses it with a papal wave of his hand.

I try to clear my head, hold my breath. Maybe I hold it too long. I feel the walls closing in. The room recedes . . .

"Is he okay?" someone says, distant.

I open my eyes, and I'm facedown on the cold linoleum floor. I see shoes shuffling across the floor. I can hear them talking about me. Their voices come from a tunnel.

"Give him some breathing room—"

"Someone call 119—"

"—I know CPR—"

Really, I'm fine, I try to say. If I could just . . .

"Check his tongue—"

"Who is this guy?"

Me, I am a seeker of truth. A hunter of Great Whites, and giant marlin, a secret lover of Emma Bovary, the long-lost third brother of Hal Incandenza. I am a giant bestriding East and West, ever the twain, with a generosity of spirit so infinite I transcend space and time. I am a prism through which all light of mankind is refracted, into rays of blinding clarity. A synthesizer of Hegelian dialectics, connector of all things unconnected. I want to go home, and sleep. I am king of all kings, Nietzsche's Übermensch, and answer to all questions and mysteries and prayers since the dawn of mankind. Home where there will be all the things I lost or forwent, everything returned. I want to go there, for there will be peace there, and rest.

"Homerrgggg," I gurgle.

"What's he saying?"

"Good God, man." It sounds like Uncle Monkey. "Get ahold of yourself."

They keep asking me for my hotel, saying it's all good, they'll just put me in a taxi. The words and numbers float in my mind, but don't settle. I can't get the hotel address out. Home is where I want to go. I can only think where I can't return.

*

When I wake up, I see the back of Minister Choi's head. I'm lying on a sofa in his office, my head propped up by a cushion. There's a low-pitched hum in the room that sounds a bit like a moan.

"Excuse me," I say, sitting up. My head feels heavy. "I'll just ..."

"Should rest," the minister says.

"*Anyo*," I say, and apologize. "*Jwesonghapnida*."

"*Kwa-yoo bool-keup*," he says. Another of his four-character sayings, nuggets of Classics wisdom. This one I think means too much is worse than too little.

"Americans speak too much," he elaborates, unhelpfully. "They speak when they should listen. Teach when they should learn."

It feels late. I look for the clock, gather my shoes.

"I hear you and my niece got along," he says, turning his chair around to face me.

It sounds like a question, and I say, "*Neh*."

The minister waits for more. But all I do is bob my head down and up and down again.

"When this sovereign bond is done," he says, "perhaps you will have more time. To get to know each other—"

"I may not be here to see it through," I blurt. "I need to go back to New York. To New Jersey, that is. Sir."

He lights up a Marlboro, looks hard at me. "Lee *Yisa*, I know you are overworked, but I do not need to tell you how crucial this dollar financing is to us, to our economic recovery. If we fail to raise eight billion, our country may not—"

"It's not that, sir. I know what's riding on this assignment. It's just, I have this personal thing to attend to . . . a family matter."

He squints at me as he sucks his cigarette.

"My *abuji* . . . he's ill. Very ill." The words come out in a whisper. "I feel like I should be with him."

The minister closes his eyes, nods. "Duty to father. I understand. Of course I do. But duty to country, that is . . . a different order. We men are all sons, but how many of us get to serve our country in her moment of need? The opportunity to show our loyalty." His eyes open, then widen. "Hanguk needs you."

"That's kind, but you think too highly of me," I say. "Any VP at Phipps could do the job. Jack could fill in—"

"Lee *Yisa*," he says, shaking his head. "If we cannot pay back the dollar loans, our economy, everything we have worked so hard for, over decades—*collapse*. Businesses go under, people, by the thousands, hundreds of thousands, out on the street . . ." He takes off his glasses. "You are in a unique position to help. Your experience, your background. You *understand*."

My head feels heavier.

"*Kamsahapnida, Jangkwannim*," I say and get up to leave.

"You have been to the Forbidden City Palace? In Beijing?"

I shake my head, sitting back down.

"At the palace, in back," he says. "There is a chamber, separate from the other 9,998 rooms. It is called the Chamber of Mental Harmonization. A small room, unceremonious, bare of furniture except a solitary wooden chair. That is where the emperor would go when faced with a big decision."

"*Neh.*"

"The emperor would sit in that chair in that room and think. Momentous decisions on matters of state, life-and-death decisions, even important personal matters. In that room he would strive to free his mind of all desire. Empty it of greed, envy, ambition, lust. Make *harmony* in his mind. Then, and only then, could he make the best decision.

"Lee *Yisa*, harmonize your mind," he says. "For the big day."

13

Early February 1998

"Deal of your career," Wayne promises when I pick up the phone. Not one to bother with greetings, or articles. "I've decided to sell Ilsung Motors, and I'm giving it to you, pardner."

"Selling Motors?" I say.

"Shhhh," he says. "Strictly confidential, as you M and A geeks like to say."

A sale of the third-largest automaker in Korea: undoubtedly a multibillion-dollar transaction, likely to be the largest in Korean M&A history. The advisory to shoot Phipps to the top of the Asia M&A league tables, the "bibles" in our industry. Not to mention a fat exclusive seller fee.

"No pitch from Phipps needed? No beauty contest among advisers?"

"Nope, and not Phipps," he says. "*You*. Because *I trust you*." He adds, "Important deal for the group."

I already have my soul-saving deal. "You know I'm working on the big-ass sovereign bond offering, right? We're a month into it, I'm barely getting any sleep as it is."

"Yeah, whatever," he says. "Just get your cowpoke ass to our HQ downtown." He hangs up.

Despite my feeble protest, I know, and Wayne knows, I can't refuse him. It's not lost on me how a deal of this size and profile would go over with the Phipps pooh-bahs. More than that, though, it's Wayne's entrusting me with what I sense is a make-or-break opportunity for the Ilsung Group and, though he doesn't say it, for him. Trust is a burdensome gift.

The Ilsung Group headquarters is located in the heart of the central business district. When Jack and I arrive, we see an old building, constructed during the Japanese occupation period, renovations and extensions patchworked over the years. The cumulative effect is of a glass-and-steel carapace welded onto the back of a giant tortoise.

Sleet falls in daggers from the forbidding sky. In front of the entrance to the building, a group of men, fifty or sixty in all, are sitting on the ground, arms locked at the elbows. They have red vests on, matching bandannas. They punch their fists in the air, shout, "Job security and fair pay!" They chant rhythmically, in unison, "Human dignity! Unity!" Most of them sit with a large tarpaulin draped over them to protect against the wet chill, and their chant pulsates over the vinyl cover.

Across the street, riot police in helmets and protective gear stand in straight columns. From where I stand, I can see most of them are kids, likely serving their military duty. They look more scared than the demonstrators.

"What's all this then?" Jack says, eyes widening.

I read the placards the protesters wave. DOWN WITH THE PARKS! ILSUNG BEFORE PARKS! DANGYUL!! Unity.

"A union protest," I say. "It looks like the Machinists Union. From Ilsung Motors."

"Oh, great," he says. "Just great."

"My father says demonstrations are the flower of democracy."

"Yeah, well, they look like pretty angry flowers."

When I was growing up in Seoul, some evenings there would be people gathered in our living room. A dozen men and women, some workers, a few college students, would come late in the evening to talk with Abuji. They called him *Sun-seng-nim*, Teacher, and talked in hushed tones about the labor *oondong*. My parents thought I was asleep, but I could hear them through my bedroom walls. The visitors talked about how the workers needed to get organized, to fight the systematic oppression by the conglomerate owners in collusion with the Park government. I remember the urgency in their voices, the sweaty desperation of their words as they discussed their struggle for workers' rights. They said they needed leadership. "*Sun-seng-nim*," they pleaded, "you must lead us." They would leave right before midnight, to beat the martial-law curfew, going as stealthily as they came.

"Freezing their asses off out here," I say, "is what they look like. Let's get them some hot coffee."

Jack follows me into a Dunkin' Donuts around the corner. We order fifty cups of American and carry them in cup-holder cartons, bunching them in each hand.

When we give them the coffee, the protesters break their chanting to say to us, "*Aigo, kamsahapnida.*" They receive the cups from us with two hands. They ask if we're with the Citizens for Solidarity activist group. We shake our heads, *Anyo.* They look from me to Jack and say, their voices filled with hope, "Then you must be with the international press?"

Before we can deny it, a murmur of excitement ripples across the throng sitting under the tarpaulin. *Wehshin*, they nod among themselves. Foreign press.

"You must publicize our story," one of the men says. "Our plight, our struggle." He has an oily, white-flecked stubble and lips turned blue from the cold.

"It's *our* company," says another, older man. "Not the Park family's. Our sweat and toil."

"Most of us, we've worked at this group our entire lives. We deserve to be treated with human *jonumsung.*" Dignity.

Others behind him shout in unison, *Jonumsung!*

I crouch down and ask the older man, "You're protesting working conditions at the factory?"

"We can take the tough working conditions," he says. "All of us are used to hard work. We're willing to make sacrifices. All we want is to keep our jobs."

They cry, "Job security!"

"Layoffs," I say, half to myself.

"We work ourselves to the bone, the Parks and management drive our company into the ground, and we suffer the consequences. With our jobs. Nearly one thousand rank and file dismissed already. We hear there's another, bigger round of layoffs coming. Rumors of a sale to a foreign company, who'll insist on even bigger cuts." His eyes well up. "How are we supposed to live? Support our families?"

I think of the labor leaders making their case to Abuji in our old home, beseeching him for help. I remember hearing him talking all night with Umma after they had left. Abuji telling her he must help; Umma worrying about his safety. I've never belonged to a union, but I know of the laborers' anger; of the smoking-hot anger at a society that fosters inequality and lets injustice fester; of the searing humiliation born of a lifetime of indignity; of the frustration of impotence in the face of a cruel and uncaring world. I've never felt hunger, but I know of their soul-sapping desperation born of imminent poverty. I'm not a father, but I think I know of their yearning for a better life for their children. Their cry is a thunderclap across the canyons of downtown straight to my bosom. I know Abuji would think I belong down here with them rather than with executives in a suite high up in the office building, discussing deals and fees and money.

The older man sees the look on my face, and he grips my hands in his. He says I must talk to the head of their union, Daehan NoChong. To get the full story.

I promise I will.

"You make a fine capitalist," Jack says, dragging me away, "with that bleeding heart of yours."

My ears pound with the demonstrators' chants as we go up the elevator. The conference room is on the eighth floor, which is really the seventh floor; there is no fourth floor in Korean buildings. Four, *sah*, sounds like the character for death.

"What a lame superstition," Jack says, trying to draw me out of my somberness.

I point to the button for the thirteenth floor. "Don't see many of those in the US."

"Bro, whose side are you on?" he says, with ostentatious concern. "You better not be going native on me."

As the elevator doors open, he says, "Now, put our war faces on, shall we?" He holds out a fist for a bump.

The Ilsung PTF team is waiting for us when we file into the conference room. The head of Group Strategy, his deputy, and the CFO of Motors. A group kept small to ensure deal confidentiality. The deputy and the CFO have their notebook computers opened on the table, which takes up most of the room. There is a small, wilting Christmas tree in the corner, over a month past its expiration date.

"Will there be anyone else?" says the CFO, looking around. He might as well ask, Any adults joining?

Jack answers, with the charm he reserves for clients, "Shane and I are honored to be serving the Ilsung Group on this important assignment." I'm just a bit impressed with the dose of Asian humility Jack has picked up, though, with him, it's hard to tell how much of it is tongue in cheek.

Wayne had explained to me the Motors venture was a vanity play by the old man, a well-known car aficionado. The chairman used to race cars in his day. On quiet Sunday mornings, Wayne said, his father would take him out in his Bugatti Chiron, the only one in Korea, and whiz around the narrow, serpentine streets of Itaewon. He never saw him so happy as when he was behind the wheel. On an owner's whim and a nine-billion-dollar loan from the group's main banks, Ilsung Motors was launched four years ago.

But Motors has become an albatross around the Group's neck, making it debt-laden, hemorrhaging cash. Now over half of the original loan is coming due, and the creditors are threatening to exercise default on Electron, the loan guarantor. So Wayne has convinced the chairman to sell Motors. To save the group, in his words.

Jack hands out presentation books labeled "Project Thunderball," the product of three near-all-nighters by us. Our M&A head, Conway, likes to name big assignments after James Bond movies. Wayne liked Thunderball better than his internal code name, Operation Triage.

"We've taken the liberty," Jack says, "of putting together a preliminary timetable and responsibility checklist, in tab one. The gate in the first month will be our own due diligence. So we know what we're selling to the buyers." To market a dog with fleas, you need to know how many fleas there are.

"We've taken a crack at the draft confi info memo," Jack continues. "The primary selling doc. Obviously, we'll need substantial input from you. Were you planning to include your financial forecasts for this year and next?"

The blank looks on the Ilsung guys' faces show they have no forecasts. They're not even projecting to last the year. The situation is more dire than Wayne let on.

I think about the laborers protesting outside in the rain. Do they have any idea *their* company is going down the toilet?

"All-righty then," Jack says, with false cheer. "Let's talk about the buyers. You can see in section three the potential buyer list, prioritized by degree of appetite for this asset. All strategics, all globals, for a deal of this size.

"Daimler-Benz of Germany, followed by General Motors of the US, and Renault of France. Toyota of Japan a long shot, given their own difficulties. As you can see, we did up a brief profile and ability-to-pay analysis for each buyer. Next to each buyer name is the name of the Phipps coverage banker for that company."

"Small list," observes the Strategy head. His head seems incongruously large for his body.

"Yes, it's a limited universe," I say. "But, remember, at the end of the day, all it takes is a single buyer."

"I have sold," Jack adds, "plenty of companies with just one buyer starting out. It's a can-do." He exudes confidence, just as we're taught, the key in any con game.

"So, what price will we get?" says the head. At the end of his day, price is all that matters.

"If I may," Jack says evenly, "the valuation is the valuation. You can see in the last section, we worked up a DCF, uh, discounted cash flow analysis, using our own assumptions in the forecasts. Also precedent transactions and public comps. Buyers will look at the various valuation methodologies, but my experience tells me their pricing will be based on an EBITDA multiple. To get the price up, though, it's critical that we create competition, or at least the perception of competition—"

The Strategy deputy raises his hand, as if he were in a classroom. "What is this . . . E-bida?" he says. A Korean American, based on his fluent English.

"*Christ*," Jack says through clenched lips. "These guys don't know how to *spell* M and A." He holds his smile.

"It's the operating cash flow of the company," I tell the deputy. "More important than net income. Think of cash flow as the lifeblood of the company."

"Yeah, when it stops flowing," Jack adds, helpfully, "you die."

The Ilsung guys look at one another.

"We also did a sum-of-the-parts valuation," Jack says. "We think your commercial vehicles division is a cash cow. Valuable on its own. If we sell it separately from the rest of T-ball, it could fetch you higher total proceeds."

"Labor union will oppose," says the CFO.

Jack shoots me a glance. "Yeah, we saw what they're like, downstairs. Probably better if we don't tell the union. Let's keep it on a need-to-know basis." He puts a firm hand on my thigh to discourage me from saying anything else.

The door swings open without warning, and Wayne pokes his head in. "Doing the Lord's work?" he says, in English. His hearty laugh fills the airless room. Pa ha ha ha.

The Ilsung team sits up straight. The head reflexively starts to brief him: "*Buhwejang-nim*, we were just going over the bloody company—"

"I'm sure," the Prince says, waving him off, "in good hands. *Soogo!*"

With that, he taps me on the shoulder and whisks me out of the room. I can feel the Ilsung managers' stares on my back.

*

Wayne brings me to his office upstairs, a formal room for receiving guests. I sit in an armchair too low to the ground for comfort; he sits in a high-backed chair fit for a doge. A male assistant brings in coffee.

"Have some," he says, dismissing the assistant with a wave of his hand. "Kopi luwak, from Sumatra. Rarest coffee in the world. Eaten by palm civets, then how say . . . crapped out."

I thank the assistant, who seems startled at being addressed, then walks out with his eyes lowered. The coffee doesn't have much of an aroma but leaves a strong taste, bitter and tangy. I tell Wayne it does indeed taste like cat shit.

"After all this," he says, shaking his head. "They want to tear us down. Us, the other big families. You know how far this country has come?"

He doesn't wait for an answer. "When I was growing up, our country's role model was the Philippines. Can you imagine? If only we could live as well as the Phils. Free market, open democracy.

You ever smell tear gas? Student demonstrations every day at university. I went to class with it in my face every day. Thanks to those crazy, no-good student protesters. I learned to wake up and love the smell of tear gas in the morning.

"All this progress today thanks to us chaebol," he says. "And now, *to-sa ku-peng*. You know, use hunting dogs for hunting and then discard them like so much garbage when they can't hunt anymore."

Wayne explains what I already know in pieces. At the heart of the chaebol model is dynastic succession. Every group passes controlling power in patrilineal fashion, from father to son to his son, from *jangnam* to *jangnam*. It's the Korean way.

"What about all the stuff they taught us in B-school," I say. "Family dynasties are the enemy of meritocracy?"

He shrugs. Like many other scions, Wayne did not have sufficient direct ownership of the major group companies, which are publicly traded and have a diffuse shareholder base. And inheritance tax is prohibitively high. So they orchestrated the handover in a "creative" way: Ilsung Corp. issued exchangeable bonds at below-market prices, and, thanks to a loan from Ilsung Securities, Wayne and his *dongseng*, Kane, purchased the securities.

"They make us jump through hoops," he says, "to retain what's ours. So, yeah, we converted the exchangeables and, voilà!, we ended up with a controlling share of the flagships Electron and Life Insurance. Right back where we started."

Bad governance and flouting securities regulations, but they could do it, because, it's rumored, the group has regulators, politicians, and media in its back pocket. "Is it true? Those rumors about Ilsung's illicit dealings with government?"

Wayne dismisses my question with a flick of his hand. He doesn't bother denying his succession scheme or even the existence of a slush fund. "Not bribery. A 'tax'—levied on us for running a business, which is mine by birthright."

"A tax, huh?"

"It's just the politics are a bit crazier this time, with a Communist president coming in. Damn politicians are playing to the public, vowing to bust up the evil, all-powerful chaebol." They're nipping at his heels, the Cerberus of politicians, creditors, and now prosecutors. Wayne needs cash, a heaping pile of it, to make the hounds go away. "Hence, the general prosecutor's investigation into the chairman's office—and me." He shakes his head. "They're questioning the legality of the Ilsung Corp. securities purchase."

"What about the labor union?" I say. It comes out in a challenging tone. "They have a say in all this?"

Wayne sits back in the chair, looks at me. "Guess you saw outside," he says, lighting a cigarette. "Chairman gives them jobs, and this is how they repay us. We give them raises every year, but it's never enough. You want equality, I say go to North Korea. I'm sick and tired of their act."

He lets out a long spiral of smoke. "We want to take care of them. Of course we do. It's just, they're . . . unreasonable. They belong to the crazy nationwide umbrella unions, and their leaders are Communists. Those guys behind the scenes, they don't want better wages or benefits for our poor employees, they want to burn the whole system down."

"Maybe they just want respect," I say. "Some recognition that you're all in it together."

"You'll never understand," he says. "You see the guys on the roof? No? Two union guys, not our employees but reps from the national organization, they went up to the roof of our building. Climbed on to the parapet where the antenna is, armed with paint thinner. To protest working conditions in our factories."

"Paint thinner?"

"Flammable thinner. Police get close, they threaten to pour the thinner on them and themselves and light them all on fire. To kingdom go. The last thing the police commissioner needs is a couple of dead protesters. So they do nothing. They've been up there for five weeks now. Right above us. Not coming down until I personally come up and get down on my knees.

"And that's not worst of it. You know they've been camped out in front of my house in Itaewon for over a month now? They chant, 'Death to Park!' all day, all night long, they throw eggs at my car, burn effigies of me. At my *home*! My wife can't even go outside. She lives in terror. They're not laborers, they're terrorists!"

"I didn't know . . ." is all I manage to say. One man's martyr is another man's terrorist.

Wayne runs his fingers wearily through his hair. He's aged in the last several weeks, white hair sprouting up at his temples.

One night back at HBS, while we were unwinding from case studies, Wayne told me his childhood dream had been to be an artist. He had always loved to draw and paint, as far back as he could remember. He took off a semester in college to go to the south of France to paint. Like van Gogh in Arles. Happiest time of my life, he said. It was *freedom*. No chairman expectations to live up to, no group responsibilities, nobody after him. Just the sun and landscapes to watercolor.

I wish I could run away from it all, he'd said. To an island somewhere . . . and just paint. Paint all day.

Then, sensing he'd created a heavy mood, anathema to him, he asked if I knew of that Patek Philippe ad slogan, "You never actually own a Patek—you merely look after it for the next generation." "Well, *c'est moi!*" he said, cheerily. "Just taking care of the business for the next generation. That's us chaebol. *Ha ha ha.*"

"You with me, right, pardner?" Wayne says now. A transparent allegiance check, which I'd resent but for his exigent circumstances.

"Yeah," I say. I'm with him. "You have my word." But does that mean going against the laborers?

"So, timetable. Need to accelerate. Getting bit more . . . time-sensitive."

"We can try to parallel-path the factory site visits in Changwon and Pyongtaek. Field two teams simultaneously, cut the DD time in half."

"Fine, if you say so. Just remember, Thunderball holds the keys to the whole kingdom."

I finish the cup of kopi luwak. Its deep bitter taste stays on my tongue.

"By the way," he says, showing me out. "You don't have any promises tonight, right?"

"Huh? Promises?"

"You know, *yaksok*. Appointment?"

"No, but I have too much work to—"

"Event tonight," he says, ignoring me. "Invited a couple of talents." Talents, I've learned, are female movie or TV stars.

"Maybe I can bring my friend Jack along. He likes—"

"No barbarians allowed in club." When he sees the look on my face, he reassures me, "Trust me. It'll be fun." *Like the good old days.*

14

October 26, 1979

For new Americans, Umma and Appa sure talk a lot about the country they left behind. We became natural USA citizens over a year ago. But the parental units are always talking in a low voice about the Dictator and Yushin Constitution, some law that allows President Park Chung Hee to have power forever. Like one of those emperors in the old days.

Sometimes they have a group of people over our house, and they drink scotch and chew on dried *ojinguh*. They discuss about politics, always Korean *jungchi*. The grown-ups think I don't know, they always hush up when I walk into the kitchen. I can tell they're talking politics by their hushed tone. They cover up the way my friends do when someone brings in the new *Playboy* magazine. I know things. Sometimes I like to be a spy. I sit quiet on the staircase and like Agent 007—Bond, James Bond—eardrop on their conversation. I hear them talking about prodemocracy protests in Seoul and Korean Central Intelligent Agency striking fear in people's bellies. They keep calling Han-guk "our country," even though they all left it. Why leave if you can't put it behind you?

Most days at home Appa is quiet, keeping to himself and his beloved piano. But whenever the people come for the group discussions, he becomes like a different person and does a lot of talking. He gives lectures, the way he used to at university back in the old country. I can tell they respect him by the way they call him *Sunseng-nim* and listen to his words. I can listen to Appa's gentle voice all day, too.

Appa lectures one gathering about "our country's cursed history." "At Yalta in early 1945," he says, in Korean, "as World War Two was nearing its end, FDR and Stalin, with Churchill's assent, agreed to make Korea an independent, unified country. Under the American aegis, of course, but, still, unified as a single country, a single people, as we Koreans demanded, and deserved."

I can't follow everything he says, but Appa sounds so wise. I spy through the staircase railings one old woman, in her midtwenties at least, staring and smiling at him in a way that annoys the heck out of me. She's like an ugly Ginger admiring the Professor's knowledge.

"But then FDR dies," he continues, "and along comes Truman. At Potsdam in July that year, Truman decides to horse-trade with Stalin and gives the Soviet Union half of Germany and half

of Korea. He just bisected the Korean Peninsula at the 38th parallel. An historic betrayal. That's how Korea came to be divided.
And stayed that way for going on thirty-four years."

"A pawn in a geopolitical game played by two superpowers,"
Ginger says, smiling up at Appa. She has such crooked teeth.

"Our cursed fate," he says, shaking his head. "For centuries a
vassal state to the Chinese kingdoms, then an annexed colony to
Imperial Japan. And now ward to America."

Appa returns all the time to his favorite topic, the Dictator.
Boy, does he not like President Park's guts. The former army
general, in his sunglasses and high-heel shoes, with some skin
disease Appa calls Napoleonic complexion. I hear Appa talk
about how the Dictator came to power in a *coup de ta*, so his
presidency is like an illegitimate child. Appa says that put a *jeojoo*, a curse, on the country. Sure, Park is making Korea modern
and less poor, with the chaebol and their big factories. "Development over democracy" and all that. But Appa says all the rice
bowls Park puts on Koreans' tables can't wash away the evil that
started his presidency and has hung over it like wet laundry on
a clothesline.

Appa gets worked up when he talks about how President
Park rules with what they call a metal fist. The Dictator crushes
on any opposition, like that activist D. J. Kim, and tortures
student protest leaders. Tortures his own countrymen! And
country kids! He controls the military, the press, and even the
elections. The once and future Dictator. He won one election
with 90 percent of the electoral vote! Appa says he and Kim Il

Sung in the North are birds with the same feather, just different colors.

President Park's saving grace is he's not greedy about personal riches, so he's a rare clean Korean political leader. But they say he's not so clean about young women, especially actresses and singers. My imagination runs away from me when people talk about that. Appa's face turns cherry red when he says the smiling American president Jimmy Carter is propping up this "monster" for his own agenda. Says as a bull work against the Communist North.

Appa tells often about a favorite student he taught at university. Name of Shin, a political studies major. Shin talked smartly in class about the "false democracy" Koreans were living in and how they have to fight for their basic freedoms. Appa had taken Shin under his wings, and they were going to fly together to great scholar heights. They wrote a paper together, titled *"Koon-joo Min-soo."* Appa explained the title to me, saying a sea's strong waters will lift a boat, but an angry sea will turn it over. The Korean people are supposed to be the sea's waters or something.

One class Appa noticed Shin was absent, and then the next and next. He was not seen or heard for a month. There were lots of whispers about what might have happened to him. Stories about the dreaded KCIA and their not-so-secret torture chamber in Namsan. Their worst guesses were confirmed when Shin returned just before finals. He had a heavy limp and bandages on his hands where fingernails used to be. I was grossed out imagining all the bad things they might have done to him. Appa said in a shaking

voice, from then on the student just had a blank look on his face
the whole time. He said Shin became a ghost in the classroom.

*

One chilly fall day, I come home from school, and there are many
people gathered, the usual faces but some new ones, too. But their
mood is not the spirited anger I'm used to but something heavier.
Then I hear it, in bits and pieces. A presidential banquet, singer
Shim Soo-bong and a coed, a Walther PPK (James Bond's gun!),
an assassination over dinner. The Dictator dead. Just like President
John F. Kennedy, who we studied in social studies class and where
I first heard the word "assassination." Killed by a psycho Commie
sniper. Except President Park was killed by one of his own men.
I learn Park was shot during dinner at a Korean CIA guesthouse
by the KCIA director Kim Jae-Kyu ("thug number two," as Appa
calls him). Director Kim was apparently upset at losing power to
the presidential bodyguard Cha Ji-Chul (thug number three), so
he killed both President Park and Cha. Park was shot in the chest
and head, and he died on the spot. At the trial, Director Kim was
asked what was his motive, and he said, "For democracy."

What a cursed family, the Parks. The president's wife killed by
a North Korea sympathizer in 1974, now him. His poor daughter,
orphaned by two violences. What will she grow up to be? Unlike
the JFK assassination, no one dares use the word assassination
for President Park. They just call it the 10.26 incident of 1979.
The *jeojoo* of the coup, a doomed presidency. Country thrown into

something called marshal law, again. A new sheriff coming soon, I guess.

I expect Appa to be happy at the death of the Dictator. The enemy of the people and all that. But instead he's somber. For the first time, he doesn't give a big lecture to the group. "A violent beginning to presidency, a violent end," he just says. "Cursed country." I don't know if he feels guilty about having his wish come true or he's more worried about the future of the country. Appa puts a large hand on my shoulder and says, "I pray your Hanguk is better than mine."

When I go up to my room, I hear the people downstairs break into singing of the Korean national anthem. *Daehan saram Daehan euhro* . . . I can hear Appa at his piano, leading the chorus. *Great Korean people, stay true to the Great Korean way . . .*

15

Early February 1998

The driver circles and circles, but he can't find the place. Wayne's chauffeur is sweating, squeezing the wheel with his white-gloved hands, craning his neck to look at the building signs. The bright lights, watery neon signs of Gangnam pass by in a colorful blur against the cloudless night. We're headed to Wayne's club, Karma, but locating it is proving elusive, because streets in Seoul have no names; you just have to know your way.

"This our first time here?" Wayne says from the back seat, his words cutting more sharply with the even delivery.

Wayne's car is a Chairman, Ilsung Motors' latest luxury sedan. The front passenger seat has no headrest; it has a pull-out compartment to stretch legs through from the back seat. There's also no rearview mirror. Wayne had it removed because he didn't like the driver looking at him in the back. The Chairman is made with a licensed old engine from Mercedes-Benz and a plagiarized S-Class body, but because it has the Ilsung name, local executives drive it without fear of retribution from the authorities. For years it was known that if you had a foreign luxury car, you were inviting a tax audit. Mercedes-Benz and BMW could never figure out why they were having a hard time penetrating the Korean market.

When we finally arrive, the driver rushes out to open Wayne's door, but Wayne opens it himself, denying the old man this small dignity after his poor driving performance.

At Karma, there's no sign, no entrance visible. Wayne stands in front of a small aperture, which turns out to be a retina scan, and a door slides open with a hiss.

Karma is a private, members-only club, membership criteria unknown. Inside, it's all black lacquer and glass, and as I walk in I lose depth perception. The walls look like deep pools of dark water. We pass an open sitting area, where Wayne exchanges a handshake with a guy, a bit younger, my guess another chaebol *samsei*. Wayne pats him on the back, tells him to come by our room for a drink later.

We come to a glass door, whereupon Wayne says, with a wink back at me, "Open *sa*shimi," and the door slides open. We have a sashimi dinner in a room, just the two of us, along with a chef who stands behind a counter and prepares the fish. Wayne lets drop he brought over the sushi sous-master from Sushi Ko in Tokyo. The sashimi is served on black plates on a black table. It's hard to taste what I'm eating with visual sensory deprivation.

We move to the next room, where a barely visible inscription over the door reads, *Lasciate ogni speranza, voi ch'entrate.* Abandon all hope, ye who enter here, if I remember from my school days. A gaggle of starlets, all young and chic, greets us. Each of them has been sculpted, scrubbed, peeled, and polished to artificial perfection.

"They all actresses?" I ask Wayne.

"Women are all actresses," he says.

I'm introduced to a Hae Sun Kim, whom I recognize from the movies. She's taller and thinner than she appeared on the big screen. Her eyes are luminous, her skin *glows*. She's used to getting stared at.

I blurt that I'm a fan, and that she's even prettier in person. She smiles, sits down between Wayne and me. Waiters bring buckets of Jacques Selosse in ice and pop open the first two bottles.

Wayne leans over to me and says, "Never tell these chicks they're pretty. No matter how hot they are. Everyone tells them they're pretty. Cut them down, play on their insecurity."

I heed his advice, try to act unimpressed. A "talent," looks to be in her midtwenties, sits down next to me. She has a dainty beauty mark at the tip of her nose, the latest fashion among actresses.

"Oppa is putting me in a movie his company is producing," she volunteers, pointing her chin at Wayne. "How do you know him?"

Just superficial beauty, I tell myself. Even if courtesy of a higher grade of cosmetic surgeons than those ministering to the room salon hostesses. I try to make a neutral remark, but it comes out as "How long have you had that nose?"

She makes a face and moves away from me.

Wayne, watching, snorts. "Relax," he says. "They're all just looking for '*spawn*.'" The girl next to him pops a strawberry in his champagne flute, and he takes a swig.

"Huh? Spawn?"

"You know, *spon*. A sponsor." He adds, "Don't worry, you're not old enough. Or rich enough." His sudden laughter that bursts like morning light onto a darkened room. It's genuine, a signifier of an unadulterated mirth, and it's inclusive, uplifting all around him.

There is a karaoke setup, with small Bose speakers placed discreetly around the room. Everyone begs Hae Sun for a song, and, after demurring just the right amount—too much, they get annoyed—she stands and takes the mike. She's a singer turned actress. A flick of the hair, a brush of the tongue across her lips. Then she sings a love song by Nami. The lyrics are of aching longing, and as she turns her gaze to me I swear she's singing to me. Her face, mythologized by the tabloids and the public, is that of just a girl wanting acceptance, maybe forgiveness. But I notice she keeps looking at Wayne, especially after one of the younger talents slides over to her vacant seat next to him.

When Hae Sun sits down, Wayne sends for his *bisuh*. His male assistant brings in a briefcase and opens it in front of him.

Wayne removes bundled envelopes, wrapped in pastel-colored, traditional rice paper, and hands one to each talent. The packets bulge. There are no cash denominations greater than ten thousand won in Korea, less than ten dollars. To curtail bribery, I was told. Hae Sun's envelope is fatter than the others.

They nod, *Kamsahapnida*, Oppa, no awkwardness, no embarrassment. There is no sense of superiority in the giving; no supplication or shame in the receiving. I sense, simply, a primitive yearning for connection in the exchange. The talents put away the gifts in their handbags, every one a Chanel quilted model, then resume their drinking and smoking.

Everyone smokes but me. Wayne smokes Cohiba Churchills, the girls all thin cigarettes. The smoke and the sake combined with champagne are getting to me, making me dizzy.

I duck out to get some air. The sky is a deep purple. I take a deep breath, fill my lungs with fresh air. I think about the absurdity of a world in which people pay money to luxury goods makers, Chanel, Cohiba, for the privilege of advertising their brands for them. Maybe this, too, is a way of connecting, bonds purchased through brands.

I go back into the room. Now there's a DJ, and the music has gotten louder, thumping, and the girls are all dancing. Hae Sun, I think, has her hands planted against the wall and swings her head side to side, techno, I'm told, the latest dance in the clubs. Wayne is seated in a chair in the middle of the room, his shirt pulled off. He has a bored expression on his face, a stogie between his teeth. He's surrounded by three girls dancing around him. They writhe, sway to the music, their mouths close to his head as if to devour him. They seem to float in the air, Goya's witches in flight. I sit to the side, look for a blanket to cover myself.

Umma used to tell me the tale of the fox-woman when I was young. She said Koreans believe ancient creatures like the tiger, the turtle, the crane, and especially the fox attain special spiritual states. If trees exist through long ages, they become coal; so the fox, if it lives long, gains powers of metamorphosis and can appear in different forms.

One day, a fox appeared in a village as a beautiful woman, dressed in a brightly colored *chima jeogori* made of fine silk. She approached a good-hearted young farmer and promised him marriage if he brought all his rice to her, and, smitten, he did. To the next young man, an earnest scholar, she offered her hand if he brought all his books to her, and he gladly did as told.

Then the fox-woman went to the young son of the high official of the village. She told him she was his to have as a bride, if only he'd demonstrate his love for her by bringing the family silver.

"Who are you?" he asked. She just smiled her coquettish smile. "Where are you from?" he demanded. She pointed to the mountains, saying, "A place beyond there." Then she knelt before him, did her most feminine curtsy.

His suspicion growing, the young man said, "Maybe you should meet Uhmuni," and called for his mother.

Upon seeing the woman, the mother growled and showed her fangs. The young woman cried out and jumped on the back of the young man and, transformed into a fox, bit him at the nape of his neck. The mother clawed savagely at the fox and pulled her off her son. The fox, bleeding and defeated, went whimpering off into the night.

The mother made sure the fox never returned to the village. She told the son she would always be there to protect him.

16

Spring 1983

I don't know what the point is to all this fucking studying. A couple years, I'm outta here, away from Fort Lee High, off in the real world. Where there will be plenty of people like me, who get me. Or if Orwell is right, next year will be end of the world as we know it anyway. Big Brother will be watching us, and we'll all be speaking double and getting tortured with rats. In meantime, I gotta be like every other good Korean American boy and study hard and come home with straight As? Fuck that. Fuck good grades. And fuck this. I just wanna read, and only the books I want, not the lame shit they assign at school. And play my baseball.

I like "fuck" in the English language. Nothing like it in Korean, maybe in any language. Just fucking satisfying to say it, and so many

139

uses. A verb, to fuck, thrilling word. It can be an adverb, fucking awesome! Also a noun, a dumb fuck. Sometimes an exclamation, *fuck!* It can be good, fuck yeah!, or bad, fuck me, or neither. Who gives a flying fuck?! As a question, what the fuck? Or, simpler, the fuck? He's fucked, not to be confused with, he's fucked up. Sometimes a name, Hey, Fuckface. Even in the middle of words, abso-fucking-lutely, de-fucking-lightful, Van-fucking-Halen. Custom cannot stale *fuck*'s infinite variety.

I can play baseball all day long. The smell of freshly mown grass and the sharp white lines painted on the diamond. The thump of the baseball hitting glove, the thwack of the bat crushing ball. The dirt and spit and leather, I love it all. Hit 'em where they ain't! Let's play two! A well-turned double play, poetic. A bang-bang play for a tag at the plate, *You're out!*, beauteous. On the field, I'm not the Asian kid, just a shortstop and pitcher. Pitching's my thing. Nothing more satisfying than blowing away big, goofy hitters with my heater, and then sneaking by a changeup, my specialty the circle change, making their knees buckle. When they least expect it.

Coach D'Acamo is a pain in my royal ass. Always yelling we swing like bitches. Can't hit the cutoff man to save our asses. Telling me to cover the goddamn base, stay off the inside fucking corner. Rides our assholes all the time. He's a class-A bastard, truly. There was this away game, at Edison, when I was on the mound, and I heard kids on the opposing team chirping "Chinkee" from the dugout. Go back to China, they chanted. Coach D'Acamo went over to their dugout and had a word with the Edison coach. They stopped the name-calling, but, fuck it, I brushed back the next two batters with high tight ones anyway. Coach came to the mound, and he had a what-the-fuck-Shane expression. He didn't even give me the usual pat on my ass as I walked off the mound.

At the start of sophomore year I got a part-time job after school. Umma's cousin, my *imo*, runs a twenty-four-hour grocery with her husband in midtown Manhattan, where Umma sometimes goes to help out. Twice a week after school I take the ferry from Edgewater to the Big City. I mop the floors, move some crates around, and shit. *Imo* has installed a salad bar because salads are "all margin." So I prepare lettuce and cut tomatoes and cucumbers. I do the job for some spending money—Appa doesn't believe in giving *yongdon*—but mostly it's so I can put down some work experience when I apply to colleges. I am "Head Vegetable Preparer" in a "specialized gourmet food retailing establishment." Umma is usually in the back storeroom chopping onions and scallions. Sometimes she comes out with tears in her eyes, from the onions, she says, and smells funky afterward.

One Friday, Ms. Wirth, a newbie English teacher at FLH, shows up at the store. She sees me at the salad bar, and I look away. Then I think, Fuck it, and I go to the counter and say, "Hi, Ms. Wirth." "Shane," she says, her eyes widening, "I didn't know . . . your family here." She gives me a look I've seen many times before, like, Oh, what a hard life you must've had, a poor immigrant's son, working all night to help the family. Working so hard to pursue the American Dream. And such a good student!

From then on, in my English papers, I mix in some broken English, leave out articles or some other corny-ass shit, and she gives me As and A-minuses. She writes in her red ink, *Your English is getting better and better—keep up the good work, Shane!* Fuck me. I suppose we all deserve what we have coming to us.

I don't know who's more fucking pathetic, Ms. Wirth or old Mr. Erdman, the head math teacher. My freshman year, I took calculus with juniors first term, blew through Mr. Erdman's advanced differential calculus with seniors second term. Start of this year, he calls me in to his office to say they've run out of math courses for me at FLH. I can't take my eyes off the tufts of white hair sprouting out of his ears. He suggests I take some courses at nearby Montclair State College, where, he says, "There'll be plenty of other students like you." Plenty of Asian kids, like me. Because fuck if all Asians aren't good at math. I tell him I'll do independent study instead. I don't tell the parents.

Appa definitely has a stick up his ass about education. Academic excellence runs in the family, Confucian scholar tradition, all that bullshit. Another word I like the sound of, BS for short. Americans and their abbreviations. Appa is always preaching, Excellence is a habit. Habit, my ass. When I get an 89 on a test in Honors Chem, he crumples up the test paper into a ball and throws it in my face. "We came to this country for this?!"

Umma comes up to my room later and sits on the bed with me. "You have to understand your *appa*," she says, in Korean. "He just wants the best for you. He sacrificed his life for you."

BS, I want to say. I didn't ask him to bring me to this for-fucking-saken country. And he never gets off his ass to do anything. "You do all the work. All he does is play his piano all day long. His goddamn Chopin." Umma just listens. She's pretty good at that, I must admit.

I point out Appa never gets on my *dongseng*'s case. He claps silly at her piano recitals. Every time she hides his cigarettes, he roars in delight and makes a big show of looking for them. He just gives her kisses, all the time. That's not even Korean, by the way. Appa treats her like a princess, a goddamn *gongju*.

"It's different," Umma says. *You're the* jangnam *of the family, eldest son. It's your duty to carry on the family name. A sacred tradition.*

Duty, my asshole. Tradition, ditto. He and all the Lees before him can take a flying jump, for all I care. For fuck's sake.

17

Early February 1998

The squash court in the bowels of the Kukje Hotel health club is a private fortress. It's an old-style court, with sturdy, wooden floors, and it's off-limits to everyone but the Park family and their guests. It smells of wood and sweat and privilege. I'd taught Wayne squash at the Shad Center back at HBS. As a way to stay in shape after we both graduated from playing baseball. He had this court built in the basement of the hotel so he could duck down to play whenever he felt like it.

We're playing for a million dollars. On Project Thunderball, we'd quoted the low end of our standard fee range for a seller advisory, half a percent of enterprise value. Wayne insisted on a "family discount." No way could he go over six million, he said. That left a million-dollar gap.

His proposed solution: "One match, one million dollars, no tears." To be settled on the squash court, as sporting men. He doesn't understand the difference between traders and bankers; he's always quoting from *Wall Street* and *Liar's Poker*.

"OK, my Gut Freund," I said, being a sporting man.

When I come down to the court, though, I see Wayne in his suit and tie. "I'm feeling a bit beneath the weather today," he says, cheerfully. "But not to worry. Games shall go on." Someone emerges from the stairs. "You remember Henry."

Why am I not surprised to see a ringer? Henry the Equerry. I always picture Henry holding the stirrups as the Prince gets on his horse. He was batterymates with Wayne on the St. Paul's baseball team, catcher to Wayne's pitcher. Henry was also a champion tennis player at Penn. He's been at Wayne's side in the Ilsung Group since graduation.

I can back out, which may be what Wayne wants, or suck it up, go through with it. For the honor of it.

I shake hands with Henry and step onto the court.

"*Les jeux sont faits!*" Wayne says, rubbing his hands together, a boy with a lollipop.

The first game is a probe of strokes, scribbled postcards home to see how you're doing. Henry's forehand shots are hammers. He hits rail after heavy rail. But his backhand has a topspin, and he runs after balls instead of lunging, a tennis habit that sends him crashing into walls. As the games progress, it becomes apparent he doesn't understand the geometry of squash, the angles and especially the vectors of boast shots.

He compensates with his athleticism, but it's not a winning strategy.

I win the first set, relying on boasts and some well-placed drop shots. I start wondering how Henry would feel if he lost this match. The cruelty of beating a ringer weighs on me.

In the second set, though, Henry becomes John McEnroe at the net and starts cutting off my shots. He plants himself at the T, the critical intersection of the x and y axes that arbitrate the game, and swats my straights and cross-courts like so many flies. He makes me cover great tracts of wooden space, while he stands stubbornly on the red T, Colossus at Rhodes. I get fixated on getting him off the damn T. Moving him off it becomes my main goal, overriding the imperative of the game score.

I start making errant shots. I jostle him for position on the T, but Henry pushes his burly shoulders against mine, doesn't give way. He guards his space jealously, and he refuses to give lets. He also has a habit of announcing the score after every point he wins. He's winning the subterranean battle of nerves.

As the squeak-squeak of our squash shoes gets more urgent, my unforced errors mount. My rails are no longer deep enough, my crosses fall short, dropping on the tin with a pathetic ping. Every opportunity, Henry hits overhead smashes. He hits them with unapologetic brute force. These shots elicit shouts from Wayne of "Ho, nice shot!" or "Too good!" followed by peals of his thunderous laughter.

By the third set, I'm spent, out of breath and any hope of felicitous shot making. Lack of conditioning makes cowards of us all. After a particularly long rally, I bend over, try to inhale some extra air. As I wipe the sweat off my palm on the glass back wall, Wayne gives me a perky thumbs-up sign from outside. I go down in defeat, two sets to one.

"Good match!" Wayne squeals, not even bothering to hide his glee. "Top notch!"

It's a spiritual defeat. If not exactly a loss of good to evil, a defeat of honest effort. I'm bowed. But I'm not dismayed, not as much as I should be. I figure Wayne needed the million dollars more than Phipps does. My mind turns to how to explain my poor fee-negotiation skills to my M&A bosses.

"You must not be amused," Henry says. "Me coming in to settle your bet, whatever it was." He puts the used squash balls in a Harrow racket sleeve. "But you have to understand him." He uses just the pronoun.

"You see, he's cursed with a life of privilege. People just see the companies he owns, the big houses, the parties. What they don't see is how everybody wants something from him. He spends his entire day fielding favors, fending off requests. Someone he went to school with asking for a supply contract, someone's relative asking for an investment, someone he doesn't even know asking for a job at an Ilsung company for his son. He turns them down, he's arrogant; accommodate, and he's corrupt.

"But I've seen him with these leeches. He *cares*. Not just for *sang-bu sang-jo*, I'll scratch your back, whatever. He actually cares about these people. He believes it's his destiny to help them.

"When my mother came down with lung cancer," he continues, "he took care of everything, unsolicited. He got her into Anderson and flew her to Houston. Put the best oncology specialists on her. Nearly saved her." He throws his squash shoes in his tennis racket bag. "I owe him for life. I'd do anything for him."

Wayne pops his head in to say, "Hey, Pilgrim, you know I would've given you the million bucks. Could've just taken it out of the Fund." He guffaws, Ha ha ha ho ho ho.

*

After the match, we repair to the sauna, a favorite meeting place of Wayne's. We're the only ones there.

"Hae Sun says hi, by the way," he says. "Gonna put her in our next movie." I wait for more, but he launches into the topic at hand.

"Prosecutors are circling," he says, wiping the sweat off his brow. "And the labor unions want their kilogram of flesh. But a successful sale of Ilsung Motors, that's the whole cake." Whole *ca-kee*. Only shot to get the cash he needs. Otherwise, he loses control of the flagship companies to the creditors or, worse, to his ambitious brother, Kane.

Wayne confirms what I've heard from Jun and others of rival factions forming among the group executives, some supporting Wayne and others lining up behind Kane. Kim *Sil-jang*, who has the chairman's ear, has been positioned as the effective casting vote. Wayne says Kim *Sil-jang's* fingerprints can be dusted into view in the development of the rivalry. Number Two knows he's out once one of the brothers ascends to the throne. For now, he sits in the middle and plays the brothers off each other for his own gain. What Koreans call *uh-bu ji-ri*.

The heat in the small sauna room is stifling, and there is a warm smell of ripening apples.

The only way for Wayne to get Kim *Sil-jang* to support him is by raising several billion dollars in a sale of Motors. The proceeds will pay back the creditors, with plenty left for the slush fund, administered by Kim.

I have my misgivings, but I'm not feeling morally heroic enough to question deeply my role in abetting Wayne in his dubious grand plan. Just giving a client strategic advice on a corporate divestiture, I tell myself.

"The key is generating competitive tension among multiple potential acquirers," I advise. "Daimler-Benz is the right buyer in strategic fit, but we have to get GM or even Renault interested. It takes two to make a party.

"What we've got to do is strike the fear of God in GM and Renault: lose Ilsung Motors to Daimler, you lose Korea, and you can kiss the huge China market goodbye." Wayne soaks it in. "All we need is one of them to be a stalking horse to Daimler," I say. "Only way to get the acquisition price up. As it is, we're concerned Daimler will hold out to pick up the asset on the cheap. At a fire-sale price." Which would be not unreasonable, since it is a fire sale. "But, no matter what, we can't look like a desperate seller."

Wayne nods vigorously; he's excited to be privy to the dark arts of M&A. He offers to plant a story saying that creditors are firmly supportive of the Group in one of the local papers he's "friendly" with. I tell him we need to leak the story to the *Financial Journal*, the influential international paper. We agree I will do it, since I know the Asia M&A beat reporter there.

Wayne says, in case I didn't get the message, "Pardner, my entire empire turns on this deal."

I nod.

"Just hope you're better at M&A tactics," he says, "than you are at squash. Or with chicks." He snickers. "You with your romances ..."

18

Spring, summer 1984

Ru, Ruth, Ruthie, light of my loins. My first, my one and only. Ru-thie. Two syllables that roll off the tongue and make my heart go, *ba dum, ba dum*. Ruthie has pale skin and golden hair, thin ropes of radiant sunshine, and eyebrows to match. She has wispy blonde hairs even on her arms! Not like Korean girls, who don't have any hair on their arms, though I can't really remember. She doesn't walk, she glides, like she's on ice skates. She's a senior, a year ahead of me, and her boyfriend, Curt, is a running back on the Fort Lee goddamn football team, but she takes interest in me. Go figure.

We're in the same AP English class. We read *The Great Gatsby* together, Daisy and ol' Sport. She tells me about the American way of reinventing yourself, how it's really possible. It's the

American way. We read Emily Dickinson and recite Walt Whitman together, singing the songs of ourselves. I get a tingling sensation every time she talks of the body electric.

One Christmas eve, right before school break, Ruthie comes up to me in the hallway and gives me a hug, saying, "Merry Christmas, Dae." Right there in front of everyone, like it's the most natural thing in the world. How downy she felt with her plump pillows in front. And Dae, not Shane. Not even Dae Joon, just my first syllable. The familiar bordering on the intimate, just between her and me. Like she knows the real me, underneath the American me. She writes her phone number, with her left hand— lots of lefties in America—on the inside flap of my Strunk & White. I stare at the flowery numerals, petals of *what if?* fancy, for days before calling her.

On our first date, we go to the movies to see *Against All Odds*. Rachel Ward rolling around on the beach, while Phil Collins wails, *"How can I just let you walk away . . . ?"* In the darkness of the theater, I hold her hand in mine. We kiss, my first kiss, and she tastes like popcorn, lightly buttered and salted. I press my cupped palm against her chest, and she guides my hand to her heart, holds it there. She leans her head on my shoulder, and I sit there not daring to move my arm. Just take in the floral shampoo fragrance of her hair. The screen flickers. *"Take a look at me nowwwww."* Ruthie whispers I have beautiful eyes. Like almonds, she says.

Ruthie teaches me to drive in her red Alfa Romeo. I wanna get my driver's license, and she's my teacher. You're not truly

American until you start driving. In the school parking lot, she teaches me to reverse, to watch the blind spot, and, hardest, to parallel park. She says to go gently, always start slow. Think of the passenger, she says. Just tap the clutch, before caressing the accelerator. Build it up, keeping a steady rhythm, let the engine purr. Be attentive and be responsive to her, that's the most important thing. Gentle, then hard. When you're sure the engine is revving, step on it, thrust, thrust, and off we go, *vrooom!* Let her fly! We hit top speed, and we both yell at the top of our lungs. You're learning, she tells me, satisfied. Gonna be a good driver someday. I think I might be a natural at it.

After one English class, Ruthie tells me she has two tickets to Bruce—Bruce, never Bruce Springsteen—and Curt has an away football game. It'll be fun, she assures me. The concert is crowded, packed with people who look like Ruthie, and they holler and smoke funny-looking cigarettes. The world has so many secrets yet to reveal to me. "*The screen door slams, Mary's dress waves . . . ,*" and Ruthie sways, like a vision.

We drive back in her Alfa convertible, top down. She lets me take the steering wheel because she's "wasted." I keep one hand on the wheel and put the other behind her on the headrest, just like cool guys do in the movies. The wind blows back our hair, the stars streak across the liquid sky. She throws her arms up and shouts at the top of her lungs, "Baby, we were born to RUNNN . . ." And she looks . . . happy. The sight makes me happy, and my heart feels full, and I'm grateful in that moment to be alive.

One day, on the school quad, I see Ruthie sitting and talking with an Indian boy, one year my junior. Her boyfriend and his buddy walk by, and the buddy says, "Look, Ruth's minority case for the week." He laughs, and I feel something crumple in my stomach. Just before I turn away, Curt looks at me and rolls his eyes. My friend is an idiot, he seems to say, and the two of us are in on the secret. Don't worry about it. I like the way Americans roll their eyes. Only Americans do that. And wink. Asians don't look right winking. Or shrugging shoulders. Especially accompanied by Why not?

There should be more Why not? in Koreans. Wish Umma and Appa would partake of that American spirit.

*

In the new schoolyear, Ruth goes off to Mount Holyoke.

A couple weeks after she leaves, I send her a long, handwritten letter. I quote a Shakespearean sonnet and every Romantic poet I know. I check the mailbox for a reply every day for a month. When she finally writes back, Ruth says how much the world has opened up to her. She's discovered philosophy, religion, psychology, sociology; no mention of literature. She "exhorts" me to consider going to a small liberal arts college, too, Amherst, Haverford, Swarthmore. Take the road not taken, she tells me, and get a proper education. And meet all sorts of interesting people. *Maybe I could even play D-III baseball there.*

It's the last I hear from her.

19

Mid-February 1998

The climb is harder than it looked from the village. The mountain is not steep, but the path is narrow, uneven, laden with jagged stones. I pause to rest, sit on a rock, and fill my lungs with the mountain air, cool and damp. I take a long pull from my thermos of cold barley water. The late afternoon sun is still strong, and I feel my shirt clinging to my back from perspiration. The trees are mostly bare, but they provide some shade. Down below, I can make out the village, a chessboard of thatched roofs.

As I climb, the air thins and my breath cuts more quickly. Finally, I reach a clearing. The light has faded, and the place is shrouded in mist. There is a single thatched hut. In front are burlap sacks and straw baskets filled with rice and grains and cinched with twine. Smoke rises, not from a stone chimney but from a pile of twigs and leaves in the front yard. The burning leaves sound like the fluttering of sparrows in flight. The smoke spirals skyward into the mist. I cross the clearing, and I see the house is old but sturdy, built of pine, darkened with age. Rice paper, yellowed in spots, covers the windows.

"*Yeoboseyo*," I say, a couple of times, each time louder.

An old man peeks out from behind the front door. His thin face has deep creases, badges of a lifetime of hard work in the fields.

He recognizes me. "*Doryungnim*," he says. *Young master*. He drops down to do a deep bow, which I stop in midmotion, stand him up. I bow to him instead.

He takes both my hands in his. His hands are callused, two large mollusk shells. "So tall," he says, revealing black space where his front teeth used to be. "Your *abuji* . . . ," he says, his voice trailing off.

His name is Yong Moon, but he is known in my family simply as Ajussi. He's the caretaker of the Lee family mountain. He looks after Eunsan, Silver Mountain, living off the land. His father was the caretaker before him, also called Ajussi in his time. I heard he had a son who had had enough of the mountain life and went off to Yonsei University in Seoul, his tuition paid for by my father. The son now works as a pharmacist in the city.

Ajussi says little, just looks at me for a long time, smiling. He smiles more with his eyes than his mouth, in the way of people used to living alone. Ajussi takes my hand, wordlessly leads me on a walk to the other side of the clearing.

There, on a gentle slope of land, lie rectangular mounds of dirt, spaced a meter apart. Some are larger than others. In front of each mound is a simple slab of marble with three Chinese characters on it, and I recognize the Lee letter on each name. My ancestors' tombs, going back generations. One of my uncles, my grandfather and grandmother, and my great-grandfather and his siblings, all buried here, side by side. There are over a dozen mounds in all. Grass and moss grow on the mounds, and they have become over the years and decades part of the mountain, as much as the trees and the streams.

I kneel on the ground, and I can feel the dampness at the knees of my pants as I do two *keunjeol*, deep bows, in front of each of them. It is the ancient rite of respect toward the ancestors, just as I was taught to do by my parents. Paying respect to a line of Lees, as Abuji often reminded me, going back over a thousand years.

Ajussi stands there, hands clasped in front. I stand next to him. It's quiet here, a stillness not found in the city. It's a quiet of distances, of great open spaces. A quiet that echoes.

"There used to be tigers in these mountains," Ajussi says, breaking the silence. He tells me of the great fearsome *horangyi*, "majestic beasts," that used to roam around here. Kings of the mountains. Their roar could be heard across valleys. People left them alone and did not hunt them, partly out of fear, partly respect. The tigers were believed to carry mystical powers. Sacred beasts, the *horangyi*. Killing one would incur the wrath of the mountain gods. "Your ancestors lived with them for generations.

Until the Japanese soldiers killed them all," he says, with disgust. "For sport."

"Your *halabuji* . . . ," he says but doesn't finish.

A story from my childhood comes back to me. I was on a walk with my grandfather on a cool evening, and I asked him about the rumors about him and our family. People said during the colonial period, Japanese soldiers in their crisp khaki uniforms could be seen coming to and going from Halabuji's house. I asked him if it's true, the stories about his working as a Japanese collaborator. Is that how we got our wealth?

Halabuji told me then the old tale of "The Grateful *Horangyi*." Once upon a time, a young man came upon a huge tiger lying groaning by the roadside. Scared but wanting to help, he asked the animal what was the matter, and the tiger roared and opened his mouth wide. There he saw a bone splinter stuck in the beast's throat. The young man bravely put his hand in the tiger's mouth and pulled the splinter out, saying, "There, all better now." The tiger licked his savior's hands and shed tears of gratitude before galloping away, his great tail swinging.

The next day, the young man went to the capital city of Hanseong to take the civil service exam. He had dreamed his whole life of becoming a high government official so that he might become wealthy and respected. But the exam was very difficult, and there were hundreds of qualified applicants who came from all over the country. He was resigned to failure and prepared to go back to his humble life in the village.

That night, the student had a dream in which a beautiful maiden appeared and said, "Do not despair. I shall repay you for your kindness yesterday." She told him: "Tomorrow a wild tiger will rampage through the city. No one will be able to stop the tiger. The king will offer a big reward to anyone who can kill the wild animal. You shall take a bow and arrow and shoot the tiger with an arrow. Only you will be able to kill the beast. I know, because I am the tiger." The student protested, "How can I commit such a cowardly act, to shoot an animal for nothing but my own glory? And how can I kill it, knowing it's you?" The mysterious girl said, "It is a reward for your virtuous heart," and vanished into the air.

At dawn, a fearsome tiger appeared in the city and ran wild through the streets, just as the maiden had prophesied. No bowman could hit the beast. Panic and chaos swept the city. The king made a royal proclamation: "Whoever kills the tiger will be rewarded with a high court rank and land and a warehouse of rice!"

The young man, who had harbored doubts, could see now that this was his destiny. He stood up on the highest platform in the main street of the capital, aimed his bow, gave it a mighty pull, and shot one arrow. The arrow whistled through the air and found its mark. The tiger dropped dead.

The grateful king rewarded the brave young man with a nobleman's title and all the riches befitting the position. But his greatest reward was the girl from his dream. She appeared before him, more beautiful in real life, and offered herself as his bride. They were married, and they lived a life of privilege and virtue.

I want to ask Ajussi if the killing of the tigers had something to do with the mountain curse I had heard about for so long.

"Lee family curse," he says. "No more breath, no more life. Your *abuji* now, his *buchin* before him. All same disease." I detect a soft tremble in his voice. "Curse. The mountain spirits. For our acts." He says no more.

Darkness has descended on the mountain, and I can hear the rustle of evening wind.

"I raised your father," he says, staring off in the distance. "From when he was a little boy. Such a gentle boy. He loved most playing in the apple orchard." He tells me of how Abuji would know exactly which apples to pick. He carried the apples in his shirt, pulled in front to make an apron, always dropping a couple on the way. In the long summer afternoons, Ajussi could always find him under the shade of an apple tree, reading a book.

We stand wordlessly for a long time.

Ajussi lets out a sigh. "They want to buy the mountain," he says. "One of the big-city chaebol. To turn it into a golf resort." He turns to me, his eyes pools of stillness. "It's yours now, *Doryungnim*. Your decision."

"Not to worry," I say. We'll never sell. Curse and all, mountain spirits be damned, we'll always keep our Eunsan, for eternity. For as long as there are Lees breathing.

"I will bring Abuji's body here," I tell him. "When it's time. To be buried, where he belongs."

Ajussi nods, as if he knew. As he has always known. "I will be here," he says.

We embrace to say goodbye, and Seoul feels distant, a world away. I assure him, I'll come back. And I start my long climb down the mountain in darkness.

20

Toward the end, Abuji lay motionless on his hospital bed for days. He breathed through two plastic tentacles extending from his nose to an oxygen tank. He gasped with each breath, clinging to the life every borrowed breath represented. Months of steroid treatment had left him a shriveled bundle of nerves and pain. The Appa of my childhood, once my rock of Gibraltar, now a form of unfamiliarity. "*Adeul*," he finally said: home. We brought him home to spend his last days with us.

It had a name, what killed him, idiopathic pulmonary fibrosis. A disease that scars lung tissue and causes progressive dyspnea, until you can breathe no more. Cause unknown, cure nonexistent. "Idiopathic" from Greek, meaning unknown cause; "pulmonary" from the Latin *pulmonarius*, relating to the lung; "fibrosis," new

Latin, a condition of fibrous, or scarred, tissue. For once, defining the words, breaking them down to their roots, didn't help me understand their meaning any better.

When Abuji was diagnosed, the doctor, a lung specialist, told us what a rare disease IPF is, discovered in only thirty thousand people a year in the United States. And how deadly. He showed us pictures of a fibrous lung, its thickened tissue blocking the airways, preventing oxygen from moving through the bloodstream to the brain and other vital organs. A disease, I'd thought at the time, that doesn't even have the dignity of metaphor: denying you life literally by taking your breath away.

The doctor asked if there was any history of IPF in the family. If so, he explained quietly, there's a ten times greater chance of getting it than someone without a familial IPF gene. Then he told us to prepare. He said the one-year mortality rate is higher than most cancers. Umma collapsed. She brought down a tray of food and bottles of pills as she fell; they clanged soundlessly on the floor. When we told Abuji, he nodded and, turning to me, said, "Don't smoke."

Those last days when I sat at his bedside at home, as Abuji drifted in and out of morphine-induced unconsciousness, my dreams and memories bled into one another. I dreamed of Abuji holding my hand on a beach, my small hand in his large hand. I saw him crumple up the report card, the one with a B+ in a sea of As, and the burn of shame returned to my face. I remembered him showing me how to throw a curveball. "That's right, son. Snap that wrist." A moment shared, lost.

I heard his laugh, gentle, ringing. I could feel the soft kiss he planted on the top of my head when he thought I was asleep. I saw his gaunt ghost at the piano, and I could hear his plaintive "Moonlight Sonata." I imagined him sitting in his study, reading his sacred texts. Do we choose what to remember, and what to forget?

When I was seven or eight, Abuji took me on a hike with my grandfather up Bukhan Mountain. Three generations of Lee men together, he said; three *jangnam*. The path was rugged, and I struggled to keep up with the adults. Halabuji stopped often—for me, I'd thought.

At a clearing near the summit, we sat down on some smooth rocks, and they had *makgulli*, milky rice wine. Halabuji, out of breath, beads of sweat on his forehead, told me, "Your father was the best student in our village." When he was accepted at Seoul National, the people in the village threw him a celebration. They slow-cooked a whole hog over a spit, and the meat was shared by everyone. "My son the scholar," he said.

"Then war broke out," Abuji added, as if that explained it all. The forgone opportunity, loss, the pain of what followed.

Halabuji stood up, breathed in the mountain air, and said, "Such fresh air ... I wish I could breathe it some more." That's when my father found out about his father's lung disease. I remembered the sadness in Abuji that day, his heavy silence on the walk down, though I didn't understand at the time. Our relentless family cycle.

At the end, Abuji lay on his bed lost in his thoughts and memories. I tried to talk to him about the life he had lived, the half I had shared with him. About the life that was the sum of our moments together, ours alone, once. I recounted to him stories of our trips together, hiking the Milford Track in New Zealand, just the two of us, riding horses in the steppes of Mongolia. The copper smell of the *ger* we slept in, the saddle sores, our guide, Nergui, who kept pushing us to go boar hunting, all remembered aloud. I wondered if he'd understood our trips were my way of trying to make amends to him, for going my way, not his.

Abuji responded mostly with silence. Once, he asked for his father, asking where his *abuji* was. Another time, he gained consciousness just long enough to reach for my hand. Mostly we sat for long stretches in shared quiet. I listened to his labored breathing. Struggling to gain a few precious last breaths. The hissing respirator, the low hum of the cardiogram machine. Even now they echo in the stillness of my mind.

"*Woori adeul*," he said at the end, looking at me. *My son.* A moment of recognition, and comprehension, acceptance maybe. Years of pain and sadness and happiness and wonder compressed in that moment. A feeble squeeze of my hand, one final breath. Then he floated away, as if pulled in a soft current. And I was left, alone.

III

I will arise and go now, and go to Innisfree,
And a small cabin build there, of clay and wattles made;
Nine bean-rows will I have there, a hive for the honey-bee,
And live alone in the bee-loud glade.

And I shall have some peace there, for peace comes dropping slow . . .

William Butler Yeats, "The Lake Isle of Innisfree"

III

21

Mid-February 1998

The Seoul Philharmonic performs Mozart Symphony No. 41. Jee Yeon is one of a dozen cellists in the orchestra; she sits in the second chair. Her torso sways as she plays, almost sensuously, with sweeps of her bow. Then she floats, eyes closed, on gossamer wings of lyrical flight. In the curve of her bare right arm, thin, taut, vibrating as she plucks music out of her instrument, is localized the sum of her graceful beauty.

Jee Yeon's grace can be liberating, I muse, for the person with her. You could be lifted with her. She could cover for your own sins and failings. Maybe make you regard the world, and your own life, with its baffling twists and soul-defeating turns, more forgivingly.

"Wonderful performance," I tell her as she comes off the stage. I apologize for not bringing a bouquet of flowers, like everyone else.

She thanks me for coming and adds, "Next time, Dae Joon-*ssi*."

Jee Yeon's family has a reception afterward at a private room at the Kukje Hotel, and Minister Choi invites me to join. Her family and friends fill the room, and uniformed waiters serve glasses of white wine. Everyone compliments Jee Yeon on her debut recital, says what a smashing success it was. And such a beautiful gown.

Minister Choi introduces me to Jee Yeon's father, Chairman Chung. The owner, I was told, of a midsize chaebol, Pyunghwa Group, specializing in defense equipment. I bow; the chairman puts his hand out for a Western handshake. I grip it in both hands and half-bow again.

"Heard much about you, Lee *Yisa*," he says. "A high financier. Hahbadeu-trained." He has full command of his thoughts and words. And his posture, betraying his military roots.

The minister already sketched his brother-in-law's background to me. A pet student of Park Chung Hee when Park taught at the ROK Military Academy. Parlayed the Park mentorship into a small defense contractor business. First ball bearings and pins for grenades. Hit the big time with tear gas. Worshipped President Park as a born leader, a true patriot. Preached Park's "economic development over that democracy crap." Believed that's just what Hanguk needed then and has made Korea what it is today.

"Still just learning," I say. "Sir."

His piercing eyes show someone used to judging. "Not just well educated," he says to DPM Choi. "Humble, too." He hands me his business card, which has two simple lines, Pyunghwa Group, *Hwejang*, or Chairman.

"Why don't you come by the office," the chairman tells me. "Talk man-to-man. Call my office—my *bisuh* will arrange it." With a heavy pat on my back that feels like a reprimand, he goes away, leaving me alone in a corner with Jee Yeon.

She stands hands clasped in front of her. Not one for small talk. When she does speak, Jee Yeon rarely talks directly; she makes me figure out her meaning by context, by the nuances of her speech, and her subtle gestures. What Koreans call *nunchi*, eye-sense.

"We're always meeting in hotels," I say.

She smiles knowingly. Your wit doesn't cover your insecurity, her expression seems to say.

"My parents," she says, in her soft, bird-like voice. "A bit 'obah.'" Overdo things. As though she's embarrassed by the hotel, the catering, all the congratulations.

"Your father . . . a bit scary," I say. "I mean, serious."

"Serious. I've heard that."

"Must've been a fun-filled childhood."

She tilts her head a touch. "Don't we all pay for the sins of our fathers?"

"Hm," I manage to say. She seems to know more than she lets on. I decide to keep it light. "Mozart, I grew up hearing it. My father on the piano. Beautiful, a bit haunting."

"You mentioned," she says. "Does he still play, piano?"

"When he can." Not an untrue statement. "He's a musician at heart. Like you."

"Musicians at heart," she agrees, with a half-sad, half-amused expression.

I notice she has a new necklace. A thin silver chain with a small pendant that looks like a silver dagger. No, a sword. Sword of Damocles? A cosmic sign. Who needs fortune-tellers? "*Eun-jang-do*?" I say, pointing.

She gives a small laugh. "My, look who's become steeped in Korean traditions," she says.

"Don't Koreans say, 'the arm bends inward'? Koreans should be Korean, be with others like them?"

"The leg bends outward," she says. "Besides, I don't need a dagger to protect my virtue."

"A sword of Damocles then?" I venture.

She looks down at her pendant. "Just a horn, I think," she says. "Sorry you had to meet my parents this way."

"They seem like nice Korean parents. Serious but nice."

Jee Yeon smiles her Mona Lisa smile, neither confirming nor denying nor revealing. I'm learning to read her intentions by what she doesn't say as much as what she says.

"Ever feel like getting away from it all?" I blurt. I gesture toward the noisy, crowded banquet room. "I mean, all this—"

Her eyes lock on mine, and before I can finish, she grabs my hand, whisks me toward the exit in the back. We make a beeline to the door, not daring to look back.

The exit door opens to a small garden, which has a path to the streets, and we run, hands still clasped, she in her high heels, holding her bunched gown in her free hand. The cold air against our faces is bracing.

"Freedom!" she shouts, breathless, and we share the giddy laugh of conspirators.

Jee Yeon has on just her white gown, her arms bare. She stands there, rubbing her arms, and beauty reveals itself, slowly, like a flower blooming in spring. I take off my jacket, put it around her shoulders.

We walk along a dimly lit side street, and she hooks her arm through mine.

"Your father's not going to be amused when he notices you missing," I say. "He'll think I'm a bad influence on you."

"We can be bad influences on each other," she says.

We come by a children's playground. She sits in the swing and starts swaying back and forth. She looks joyful, like the carefree girl I imagine her to have been growing up. As she swings toward me, the faint moonlight catches a hint of sparkle in her eyes. Her subdued beauty, there the whole time. Could this woman be the yin to my yang that I've been looking for? I want to believe a boy and a girl can bridge cultural divides infinitely better than countries can. After all, isn't that the metaphorical nature of love, making a connection of differences?

"I need to leave soon," I say. "After I finish some business with Wayne. You know, of Ilsung? Then I have to go to London, before going back to New Jersey to see—"

"Wayne, of Ilsung?" Jee Yeon says. "Park Hyun Suk?"

"Why," I say, my voice catching, "you know him?"

She lets out a sigh. "We all know each other. Small society."

"Know, how well?"

"We went to CIC together when we were kids," she says. "Children's International Community, a silly gathering for kids from bourgeois families, mostly chaebol. We were at Vienna together one summer. That is, my parents sent me. Energetic kid, always looking for fun, and mischief. When we hit high school, several of the CIC kids' mothers formed a *kwaweh* group, for private tutorials. Hyun Suk was one of the kids in our group."

"Huh. So you must've known him pretty well."

"Guess you could say that. In those days, private lessons were outlawed. President Chun's lame attempt at showing a level playing field. Equal opportunity in education, rich or poor. Our mothers had different ideas, of course."

"*Binik-bin booik-boo.*" The poor get poorer, the rich richer.

"Something like that. We did *kwaweh* in Yongpyeong, three hours out of Seoul, to escape detection. At Hyun Suk's winter house there. Five of us, three girls, two boys. We did calculus and then English, rotating in the teachers. Hyun Suk was naturally smart but . . . casual about his studies. Rarely did his homework, but when we had problem sets in class, he'd be the first one done. And he'd make a show of getting up and doing other stuff, singing, watching TV, while the rest of us were sweating over our problems. The other two girls competed for his affections. It made for some amusing sessions."

"Sounds like the Wayne I know."

"To unwind after studies, we'd go skiing at Dragon Hill and once in a while go to the nightclub there, the Pointe, think it was called." She shakes her head at the recollection. "One night there, this waiter, a bit older, started in with us, stirring up trouble. Kept saying under his breath, loud enough for us to hear, "Spoiled little brats. Think they own the world." Just mad at the world, I guess. He decided to take it out on a bunch of wealthy-looking kids. We tried to ignore him, but I could tell Hyun Suk's patience was wearing thin. Then the waiter leaned in on one of the girls and said, "What you need is a good spanking. You want me to give a spanking, *gongju?*" At that Hyun Suk rushed him, and they got into a scuffle. The other waiters joined in, must've been six on two. Hyun Suk and the other boy got beat up pretty bad. Bloody noses, bruises all over their faces."

"What then?"

"We all got taken down to Yongpyong police station. We were scared out of our minds. Underage drinking, fighting, getting arrested. What're our parents going to say? Hyun Suk stood up—he had this thin cone of reddened Kleenex sticking out his nostril—and announced to the police supervisor he had started the fight and he would take full responsibility. He told the cop to let the girls and the waiters go. We were relieved; the waiters were just stunned. He'd taken it all on himself. For the lot of us. That's the Hyun Suk I remember. Anyway, think he went for *yuhak* shortly thereafter, to a boarding school in America."

Seeing me lost in thought, Jee Yeon asks, "Your problem, the *gomin.* Something to do with him?"

"I shouldn't really talk about it," I say. "Need-to-know and all that. But I am caught between two choices."

"Scylla and Charybdis."

"Between someone who's entrusted me with something important and some helpless people who desperately need my help."

She waits for me to continue.

"Okay, you've probably guessed that someone is Wayne, uh, Hyun Suk. The other group is the laborers at his company, Ilsung Motors. Doing what Wayne wants may hurt the workers. But these workers . . . I saw them protesting, and it . . . I never saw anything like it . . . Like their life depended on it.

"I'm not sure what they want, the workers, their labor union. Wish I knew more. To see if I can help them. It feels *important*." I look up. "I wouldn't expect you to understand."

"You'd be surprised," she says. She lights a cigarette. "I might know someone. A *sunbae* from my student demonstration days."

"You used to be a protester?" I say, a bit more loudly than I meant to. "You marched and got teargassed and all that? Thought you went to Ewha to study the cello."

"My freshman year at Ewha, I won the Vienna Cello Concours, and I got a scholarship. I think you know there are no need-based grants in Korea. So I secretly turned over my grant money to my classmates who needed it. Umma was not amused when she found out." She takes a puff. "Then . . . then I had a political awakening."

I pause to let her elaborate.

"Not much to tell," she says. "A *sunbei*, a senior, took me to a campus forum my sophomore year, at Seoul National. He said it was for some community service. It turned out to be a student activist gathering, where this SNU Law student Lee spoke."

I sense she has more to tell, wait for her to continue.

"His words lit my body on fire," she says, her voice changed. "He stood on a desk and railed against President Chun Doo Hwan, his authoritarian rule. The *passion* of Lee's demand for individual rights and freedoms, basic human decency, I had never seen anything like it. That was the tinder. Others, too, they talked about real things. Important things. Real democracy, free and direct elections, free speech.

"All of a sudden, my life, the mansion, the cello lessons, all of it, just seemed frivolous—"

"That's how I felt," I interject, "when I saw the protesting laborers."

She nods. "I felt ashamed of my privilege. I renounced my background, joined the underground movement."

"I don't think privilege," I say, "is a cloak you can just take off."

She gives a long sigh. "Didn't think in those terms then. It was a heady time, exhilarating. I felt like it was what I'd been searching for my teenage years, the answer to that ache I had. I stopped going to class. Marched in every demonstration I could. We were changing society. I only just escaped getting arrested on two occasions."

She stamps out her cigarette. We stay in silence.

"This *sunbae* I know, he's someone I used to trust with my life. I heard he's now at Daehan NoChong, the nationwide umbrella organization for I believe the Machinists' Union . . . Jung Ha *hyung*, Yoon Jung Ha. If it's helpful, I can give you an introduction."

"It might," I tell her. It just might be what I need.

Her offer feels like a gesture of intimacy, reciprocating my deal-breaching confidence. I pull her close, breathe in her fragrance, try to fill my lungs with her essence.

Jee Yeon's mystery is opening up to me, a fiercely held fist slowly unclenching, one finger at a time. Our lips press, and desire tickles to life, delicious in its delicate growing touch.

Gomin no more; I can see now. A picture of a future, together. With someone with grace, who sees the world as I do, even from a different perspective. I may be running out of time, but for the first time in a long while, I see the future.

22

December 1989

Senior year, winter of my discontent. Four years spent muck-
ing around in semiotics and epistemology, entelechy, eschatol-
ogy. It feels now like so much suppurating academic *dwenjang*.
All those late-night, weed-inspired debates about who had the
greater influence on Marxism, Kant or Hegel, or which better
captures the zeitgeist of our times, *Bright Lights, Big City* or
Less Than Zero? A chthonic miasma of intellectual magma and
smegma. Important events are happening outside of campus, out
there in the real world. Life-changing, tectonic plate–shifting,
historic shit! The tides of human history are changing. The outside world beckons.

The Berlin Wall collapses, and people are celebrating the
world over. Cold War over, Reagan's triumph over the Evil

Empire. Francis Fukuyama says it's the "end of history." The end point in man's ideological evolution, American liberal democracy as the last form of government. Monarchy, bolshevism, fascism, socialism, all tried and failed, and now the final Hegelian synthesis. QED; tie a bow around it! Ironic, just a bit, that a scholar of Asian descent is so US-centric in his worldview.

Does he and everyone else forget the Tiananmen Square Massacre that happened just a few months ago? Thousands of prodemocracy protesters, most students, killed by Chinese soldiers. Premier Deng Xiaoping might have a different view on reaching the historical end point. "It doesn't matter if a cat be black or white, so long as it catches mice." How about the Gwangju Massacre a few years back, when hundreds of prodemocracy protesters, most students, were killed by Korean soldiers? History certainly does rhyme. More Machiavelli at work than Hegel. Asia's political evolution goes on.

Asian leaders might have something to say about liberal democracy's being the be-all and end-all. For them, for Asia, history is not over. It's merely the pendulum of history swinging, back toward the East. Asia, led by China, reigned supreme a thousand years ago. Now it's returning, driven by demographics, renewed economic might, and a unifying (nonreligious) Confucian ethic. Maybe American-style democracy and economic prosperity do not go hand in hand. Could be that freedom of speech and individual liberty are a by-product, not the cause, of economic prosperity. As Asian countries strive for prosperity, Chinese-style communism may prevail, or, more likely, the centralized political systems and planned economies of Japan/ Korea/Singapore/Taiwan/Hong Kong become established as the model of success.

If wars and conflicting ideologies are behind us, there looms still a clash of cultures. Asian culture, broadly defined, is not only different from but fundamentally at odds with Western culture. Civic order and economic development come first, before individual liberty. Blasphemy to Westerners, but Asians do not consider individual freedom paramount; group harmony and social order are deemed more important. That this belief may be a manifestation of what Engels calls "false consciousness" is beside the point; Asians believe in it. Americans comprehend the concept that liberty is not the ultimate ideal about as readily as Christians accept the possibility that God does not exist.

Asian societies also draw their power from homogeneity in race and ethnicity, not diversity. Asian political systems may be more sustainable in the long term because, for the most part (an exception being Indonesia), they're secular. Not separation of church and state; there is no prevailing church. Just the state and then family as the next binding societal unit. No religion to intermediate or to detract. America, like Christianity, is exceptionalist—City on a Hill?!—exclusionary ("with us or against us"), and proselytizing. Asia, as reflected in Buddhism, is inclusive and inward-looking. (Insofar as you're able to look and don't get reincarnated as a rock.)

The imminent clash will lead not to military conflict or ideological confrontation but to trade battles and economic wars. That places the markets squarely as the next critical battleground. If you think about it, all the important events and developments in the post–World War II world have been economics-driven. From the rise of Communism across Eurasia and the advent of the OPEC cartel to the formation of the European Union and the fall of the Berlin Wall and collapse of the Soviet empire. Closer to home, the eighteen-year reign of terror of President Park Chung Hee in Korea, built on the shiny promise of prosperity. Economics is the new engine of history.

The United States has played a dominant leadership role in this modern order. It has practiced economic as well as geopolitical hegemony, in the guise of a Pax Americana, in a newly unipolar world. Importantly, it has also exercised its powers from a multidimensional power base, which gives the United States a mandate unique among global leadership contenders, possibly even among historical global leaders. The country is not only an economic and military powerhouse, but also the leader in technology, sciences, arts, high and pop culture, sports, education, and, arguably, moral authority. Of these dimensions of influence, education may be the most important and of lasting consequence. America takes in the best and the brightest from around the world to its universities, the most advanced in the world, and teaches them the American way. Not just impart to the students how to build particle accelerators or run discounted cash flow analyses, but inculcate in them the values of a liberal democracy, an open society, and a laissez-faire economy. When these leaders-in-training repatriate to their home countries, they spread the American gospel. This is the power of the United States today.

Ergo, I decide: A) if the markets are the heart of the world order, then Wall Street is the epicenter, and that's where I shall play. And B) I shall pursue finance as a means of bridging the yawning divide between the United States/West and Asia/East. My manifest destiny, crystallizing. For all the world, and Abuji, to see.

23

March 2, 1998

The usual hum of the Sterling trading floor in London is amplified by a buzz of anticipation. It's D-Day, pricing day for the ROK sovereign bond offering. People move differently when urgency is joined with purpose. The trading floor is the size of a baseball field. On row upon row of white Steelcase desks, computer terminals show multiple Bloomberg screens, colorful petals of the flower of capitalism in full bloom. We join the crowd of Mop, Phipps, and Sterling people around the fixed-income syndicate desk. Director Suh and his team, the Monkey, Gandalf are all here in the eye of the storm.

We're exhausted from a whirlwind marketing roadshow that took the team from Hong Kong, Tokyo to New York, Boston, LA to Frankfurt, Paris, and London. A ten-day Escher loop of hotel-limo-office-limo-Gulfstream-limo-hotel. Group luncheons and one-on-one meeting after meeting with major institutional accounts. All to drum up interest in the bond offering. At every stop, the Mop officials insisted on Korean food for breakfast and dinner. Jun's main job as road manager was finding and booking restaurants named Shilla across three continents.

We are about to discuss the final book of demand when an announcement comes over the office PA system. Sterling CEO Dillon Merrick is pleased to announce, in his posh Queen's English, that Sterling Brothers has merged with the Umbrella Insurance Group. "A merger that will create a one-stop financial powerhouse and cause a sea change in the industry."

A heavy hush falls over the trading floor, like a tarp thrown over a baseball diamond. The Sterling employees are in shock. They freeze midphone conversation, cover their mouths with their hands. They rain down f-bombs, of the *fuuuuuuccckk* variety. It's not clear whether Sterling is merging with or being acquired by Umbrella, but everyone feels the tectonic plates already moving beneath us.

Suh leans over to ask me what this means for the pricing. "We'll see" is all I can muster.

It takes the Monkey to jolt the syndicate managers out of their daze. "The show must go on," he chirps.

The head of Sterling's International Syndicate is Phil "Fuck-face" Purell, an American and ex-Marine. He has a crew cut, a muscle-roped neck, and shirtsleeves that are always rolled up. He calls everyone outside of his syndicate desk Fuckface. The Phipps counterpart, Ike Davis, is redheaded and also an American. He has made a rare appearance, stepping off his desk at Phipps to conduct the deal pricing jointly with Fuckface.

Last night, the two of them advised the Mop officials that "pricing should be inside Malaysia," a BBB+ credit issuer. This despite ROK's S&P rating of BB+. Market "sentiment" was improving, and they felt "comfortable" that we could have tight pricing at, say, 350 basis points over LIBOR for the ten-year bonds. But early this morning, Moody's announced it was not changing ROK's credit rating outlook to *stable*; it would stay at *negative*.

Now Fuckface and Davis, fierce rivals who despise each other, are allies, and they present a united front. They say the preliminary pricing from yesterday is off the table in the face of the Moody's news. We're now looking at more like 375 basis points over. There's too much turmoil in the Korean markets, too much political instability in Seoul—and then there's the Dear Leader, who just tested an ICBM capable of carrying a nuclear payload. So pricing looks more like Brazil, a BBB− credit (barely investment grade), which had issued paper the week before at 380 over.

Director-General Yoon, just flown in from Seoul for this session, explodes. "What you talk about?" he shouts, in English. I notice his hair is more aggressively black than before. "You say we have over 80 billion dollar in demand. NO, no way we go so wide."

"That was yesterday," Fuckface says. "This is the reality today."

"Market is king," the Monkey says, unnecessarily.

"You lie, you cheat," DG Yoon shouts. "You are very shit people!" He rants, calls them every nasty name he knows in English and Korean. A vein in his forehead doesn't just bulge—it *pulsates*.

But the two-headed syndicate monster refuses to budge. "This is the right price," they say evenly. Neither bats an eye. They think they have the issuer over a barrel: they're betting the Korean delegation cannot afford to go home empty-handed.

Director Suh suggests we withdraw to discuss among ourselves and regroup in a bit. As soon as we step inside a glass-walled conference room, Yoon launches into a Korean-style scolding of Suh.

"What you do to our country?" he fumes. "For shame! Your incompetence is going to ruin all of us."

Suh just takes it; he's used to outbursts from his *sangsa*. I'm the only banker allowed inside the room. He calls me over and calmly says to go over the price sensitivity in the revised demand book.

Yoon paces the room, smoking, in front of the No Smoking sign. "*Im-jun moo-tweh*," he says, over and over. No retreat, no surrender. "We beat them with our sheer willpower." The Blue House back home has given him secret instructions to do a deal at any cost, as Suh confided to me, but he can't help himself. His Korean fighting spirit takes over.

After scrubbing the demand numbers, I make a suggestion: why don't we go back and ask the syndicate heads how much demand they think we have today at 355 over?

Suh says fine idea, volunteers me to do the asking.

Here, the lines of allegiance cross. As the investment banker, I act as the Mop's advocate, whereas the bond salespeople on the trading floor are surrogates for their clients, the bond investors. In theory, Syndicate sits in the middle and matches supply with demand, but inevitably Syndicate leans toward the investors, with whom they work day in and day out. So while Davis and I get paychecks from the same source, we're on opposite sides in this discussion.

We get back out on the floor, and I inform the two syndicate heads, "The client would like to know how much quality demand there is at 355 over."

"Fuck off," Davis says.

"They have a right to know," I say evenly.

"Who's this fuckface work for?" Fuckface says.

"Let the professionals handle the pricing," Davis says.

I go off-piste: "If there is not eight billion but less, say, five or six billion, then . . . they may be forced to consider downsizing the offering."

I've hit the nerve. A smaller offering size means lower fees, and everyone gets egg on their faces. On the Street, size matters. Prestige is measured by deal size. The Mop team has gathered behind me to watch, though keeping a few feet of distance. I see a twinkle in Suh's eye, just sheer panic in Yoon's.

Davis shoots the Monkey a look, and the Monkey aims lasers at me. Fuckface is about to call me a fuckface when Davis puts a hand on his shoulder. "Let us sharpen our pencils," he says.

They keep us waiting for an hour, though it feels longer. In the conference room, Yoon puffs through nearly an entire pack of Parliaments. I think about all we went through to get here. Have I brought the Republic of Korea, with my reckless act of brinkmanship, to the precipice of disaster? What would Abuji say if he were here? I block the thought from my mind. Out on the floor, above the trading desks, there's a large electronic display with stock tickers in bright green flitting across, and I imagine the display turning into a deus ex machina. Come to save all our asses.

When they come back, Fuckface and Davis have serious looks on their faces. Davis speaks first. "We're prepared to set it at 355.5 bips," he says. "It's an aggressive level, but we'll push our accounts. For the full eight billion. We know ROK needs . . . uh, wants the full proceeds."

"We'll have to wait till New York opens," Fuckface says, "to bounce it off a dozen top accounts. But I think we're there."

"Let us break so the client can discuss it," I say. "If we can't justify this to the Korean people, we can't price the deal." I avoid meeting the Monkey's eyes.

We go back to the smoke-filled conference room. The Mop guys pretend to agonize, even go through the motions of arguing among themselves. But they're doing silent high fives. It's eight billion in desperately needed capital, obtained at a tighter spread than anyone thought practicable. A good deal. A lifesaver for Korea.

We go back, and DG Yoon says, ceremoniously, "We have a deal." He shakes Davis's hand, then Fuckface's.

Handshakes all around. Including the Monkey, who smiles through bared teeth.

"Okay, let's get this done," Fuckface says, turning back to his phone bank.

"Ike, I just want to say—well done." I extend a hand to him. "No hard feelings."

He stares at me, then says, "Let's not suck each other's dicks just yet."

As we wait for New York to open, I hear Yoon paying the Monkey the ultimate compliment. He tells the Monkey he's so tough he must have some Korean blood in him. Heh heh heh.

I steer clear of the Monkey.

*

I duck into an office to call home to share the news with my parents.

When Umma answers, her voice is a pitch lower than usual.

"What's wrong?" I say. "Is he okay?"

She hands the phone to Abuji. I wanted to tell him all about the deal that saved Korea—the deal his son made happen! I want to share all the sordid, glorious details, how we snatched victory from the jaws of defeat. How I found the *aegukja* in myself to trump the disciples of mammon. But when I hear his labored breathing, I can't find any words.

"Adeul," he says. He tries to master his breathing. "Don't worry about me . . . Fine . . ."

I think back to the time I started at Phipps, and Umma and he visited me in Manhattan. I took them to Lutèce. My treat, I said proudly. Abuji coughed all through dinner. He downplayed it, saying, "Guess I'm allergic to New York." There was so much to tell him about that evening, all the exciting, important deals I was working on ("More to tell, but they're strictly need-to-know"), the talented, switched-on people I was working with. He listened patiently.

In keeping with Korean custom, with my first paycheck, I had bought gifts for them, an Hermès scarf for her and a leather watch strap for him. It was for his old Patek Philippe chronograph. He didn't say much when I gave it to him, just smiled. But whenever I saw him after that, Abuji always had that old Patek with the new brown strap on his wrist.

Umma comes back on. "Adeul, he keeps asking for you, even in his sleep," she says, her voice a whisper. "You'll come see us soon?"

I tell her it's hard to hear her with all the clamoring on the floor, but I'll visit soon, I promise.

After I hang up, I sit still for a long time. I am alone with my victory. The sound of a forlorn tree falling in an empty forest.

Outside the room, I can hear the whoops of self-congratulation and triumphant backslapping amid the dull roar of the trading floor. DG Yoon is calling me over, but I hold up my hand. There's one more call I need to make.

Jee Yeon picks up after two rings—as if she's been waiting. She asks gingerly about Abuji, whether he's better. I can't get the words out. I close my eyes, try to control my breathing.

I manage to tell her I'll be in Seoul next week. "I was wondering, do you think we might have dinner?" Something to look forward to, even as I look back.

24

July 1994

You can see forever in the steppes of Mongolia. So our guide, Nergui, tells us. Abuji and I are in the steppe outside of Ulaanbaatar, and in the distance the expansive flat of land merges with the sky, forming a continuous line to infinity. This is what peace looks like.

We are in Mongolia on a bonding trip, father and son. Business school behind me, my last break before reentering the world, this time for good. A peace offering, for all that has gone unaddressed between us.

We ride our horses for hours in wordlessness, under an endless, cloudless cerulean sky. We ride across the verdant grassland, galloping, then trotting, over hills and across streams. After a while, the sounds of nature settle into a stillness that echoes from the ages. The rhythmic thump of the horses' hooves. The gurgle of running streams. The sough of the wind passing our ears.

We ride for miles without seeing another person. Gazelles run by us on spindly legs of trembling grace. Once, a wild boar rumbles across our path. Nergui, riding without a saddle, frequently falls asleep on horseback, which I didn't think possible. The boar's snorts jerk him awake, and, pulling out his old Kalashnikov rifle, he says let's chase after it. What a feast it'd make for dinner. Abuji distracts him by asking about Genghis Khan, our common ancestor.

"We have *Mongo banjum* to prove it, our mutual ancestry." He turns to me for help.

"Mongolian spot," I tell him. "You know, the blue birthmark on your butt you're born with."

"Koreans, too?" Nergui explodes in laughter. "We same children of the Great Khan then." The Chairman Mao cap sits always slightly askew on Nergui's head. His name, meaning "no name" in Mongolian, he says was given to him to mislead bad spirits. He tells us, in his rumbling English, of Genghis's great conquests in the thirteenth century.

"Temüjin, mean 'of Iron,' was born a fearsome warrior," he starts. "They say he was born holding a blood clot in his fist, a sign he was destined to be great ruler." Temüjin was a born leader, and he inspired undying loyalty from his followers. By his early twenties, he had consolidated the steppe confederations under his banner. But his destiny was outside conquest.

"They gave him the name Genghis," Abuji says, encouraging Nergui. "Universal Ruler, right?"

"That's riiiiight," Nergui says, nodding in approval. "Genghis went west, conquering land after land." His military brilliance was surpassed only by his ruthlessness. The Mongol Army wiped out the mighty Khwarezmid Empire, including the entire ruling family, for breaking a treaty. In Central Europe, he laid waste to what is today Ukraine, Poland, Hungary, even some parts of Germany. Everywhere he went, the Mongol hordes left terror in their wake. Their cavalry-based army of small riders on short, nimble horses crushed the heavy armor-clad knights of Europe.

"You know Blitzkrieg, Nazis?" Nergui says. "This was first 'lightning warfare.'"

"We have saying for that, too," Abuji says. "*Sok-jun sok-kyul.* Fast war, fast victory."

"Riiiight. True, Great Khan cruel, but he led Mongol people to glory."

"Genghis was first ruler," Abuji says, the historian in him coming out, "to connect East and West. He brought the Silk Road under cohesive rule, bringing communication and trade from North Asia into Muslim Southwest Asia and Christian Europe. At its peak, the Mongol Empire under Khan stretched from China to Central Europe to Southwest Asia to modern-day Pakistan."

"Largest empire in history," Nergui says, pride in his voice. "Before death in 1227, Genghis became supreme god of Möngke Koko Tengri, Eternal Blue Sky."

His horseback hagiography finished, our guide takes a swig from a bottle of Genghis Khan vodka he carries in his sack. He asks us if we want to buy some Genghis vodka from him, best in Mongolia, not like the old Soviet yak piss.

A *ger* comes into view, smoke puffing out of its thin chimney. Mongolians are a nomadic people, Nergui tells us, and they rely on the kindness of strangers. We go inside the *ger*, which, with a dirt floor, is little more than a tent with a fireplace. A woman and her young son greet us warmly, like long-lost relatives. The crags in the woman's face bear the age of the steppes. Our hostess serves us goat's milk and cured yak meat. Nergui shares his vodka with her.

At night, under a blanket of luminous stars, we build a fire. The burning twigs crackle. The fire warms our hands, and the light from the flames illuminates Abuji's face, revealing lines of wisdom along with, I imagine, secret pain. For as long as I can remember, Abuji has maintained a fierce silence about his life. The arc of our dialogue has always bent, as seemed natural, toward me. About his hopes and aspirations for me, my desperate struggle to meet his expectations. A quiet judgment of me, when it came to it. It's never been about his own dreams and aspirations and disappointments, buried, I suspect, deep in his memory. But out here in the infinity of the steppe, at a point contracted from eternity, answers, dark, concussive, seem willing to be surrendered.

"Do you miss it, Abuji?" I ask. "The homeland?"

"I try not to," he says, in his low voice. "But I miss it. In my marrow."

"Why did we leave?" A question that has hovered over my life for nearly twenty years. Were we leaving something behind, or looking for something new?

"When I was in the army, I was a true believer. I thought Park Chung Hee was the leader who'd lead us to light, our Genghis Khan. Not just to economic prosperity, but true democracy, corruption-free and real rights for the people."

I wait for him to continue, open up some more.

"After the craven president Syngman Rhee, a US puppet, and the hopelessly inept Yun Posun, our country was lost, headed inexorably for slow ruin. We were in dire need of a strong leader to set it right. Brigadier General Park inspired fiery loyalty from the officers—from all of us. In 1961, I supported Park's 5.16 coup d'état. He'd make our country a shining beacon of hope for all developing countries of Asia. He'd bring not just development, but true democracy."

The light from the fire flickers across his face. "I was recruited personally by Brigadier General Park to join Army Intelligence. In those days, before Korean CIA came to power, Army Intelligence was the nerve center for government's operations. We gathered intelligence, analyzed, monitored sympathizers, did everything to keep the Communists out. To keep our country strong.

"Once Park got used to power, though, things changed. *He* changed. Maybe power does that. The imperative went from making the country strong to making himself strong. Think Park made himself believe it was one and the same. Sure, he did good things for the economy, especially in the first few years. He raised the people up, fed us food as well as national pride, and got us united in working for a prosperous future."

There's a bitterness in Abuji's tone I haven't heard before. "But then he started using us in Army Intelligence to track his political opponents. Not just the opposition leaders Kim Dae Jung and Kim Young Sam, but also intellectuals and students. He had us spy on our own people. Someone, I think it was Graham Greene, said that intelligence agencies are the only true measure of a nation's political health, the expression of its subconscious. Park started developing the KCIA as his own secret police. They hunted dissidents, students, anyone who dared voice opposition to the president. They rounded them up and tortured them, in the thousands. Park was Genghis, but without the vision and virtue, just his ruthlessness.

"Then in 1972 came the declaration of martial law and Yushin Constitution of October, giving him absolute power indefinitely. That was it. My conscience wouldn't allow me to continue. I filed for my discharge. When he heard, President Park himself summoned me to Blue House. He gave me a lecture on Meiji Restoration of 1868. How it modernized Japan by restoring imperial rule under Emperor Meiji and launched the country on a modernization drive and cultural and social renewal. That's what Yushin was, a renewal. Park said he needed all the good men to support him in this noble cause. But by then, I saw who he was, what he'd become: a monster. He'd destroy my country, after vowing to save it. I felt betrayed. Betrayal, that was worst part of it. I couldn't bear it."

I remember Abuji in our backyard, burning his uniforms and medals of honor.

"I got my honorable discharge and went into academia. I wanted to get as far away from the military as possible. So I became lecturer at Seoul National, teaching political history. But then the student protests started. One demonstration after another, they spread from one campus to another, across the country. Whenever momentum appeared to be building for nationwide protest, Park would make up some spy threat from North Korea. Lawmakers, intellectuals, professors, students were taken to Namsan, then Namyeong-dong, the dreaded KCIA black site that housed the torture chambers. They kidnapped DJ Kim in 1973 and tortured him for months. My own student, Shin, also taken to Namsan. Waterboarding, sleep deprivation, electric shock, tooth and fingernail extraction. Now, these were methods I'd researched and helped to refine in intelligence, studied and came to despise. I had blood on my hands . . ."

Abuji closes his eyes. "I had to leave, get out of Hanguk. They put me under surveillance, tapped my phone. They tracked all my meetings with students and labor leaders. But that wasn't it. It was my past, I had to escape it. The Dictator, intelligence, the oppression, the violence, the torture, and my hand in it, all of it. It haunted me. The blood on my hands, the guilt, the shame. Your *umma*, she's the one who suggested a clean break, a fresh start somewhere far away. She cabled her cousin *unni* to invite us to America. That was it. That was eighteen years ago . . ." His words trail off in a sigh.

I ask if he wants to. Return.

"I can't. Some things you can't get back."

Are fathers unknowable to sons? We grow up familiar with the shape of our father's hand and the timbre of his voice, we learn to measure his pleasure or dissatisfaction with our latest accomplishment. Yet how little we know of his once-soaring hopes and roaring ambitions, his hot-breath desires, unsated yearnings, and the compromises and capitulations that hang from his life like dried-up grapes on a vine.

"Do you regret it—any part of it?" I say.

"Sometimes. Sometimes I think about what might've been. To have continued the fight . . ." He looks up. "But I had you. And your *dongseng*. I wanted my children to grow up in an open environment, knowing true freedom. To live without fear, without baggage. So we came to America, the land of fresh beginnings, where you could be free, to study and learn. To be good, wise people."

Freedom, to be what I want to be? Not bound by the yoke of family tradition or the even more chafing shackles of a father's expectations? Pursue what I want to do, be my own person? Yes, that would be freedom. Maybe sons are unknowable to fathers, too. We are of their blood and issue, but how much do they really know us, want to see and hear us? Do they hear our furious cry for independence?

I had expected pride on Abuji's face when I walked across the podium in Harvard Yard to receive my MBA diploma. I had studied hard, earned Baker Scholar distinction. Instead, I saw disappointment, masked by a blank expression. Because it was not a PhD diploma in the Yard or a *byustle* for a high-ranking position those Lees of yore received? Because the greatness, in all its splendid possibilities, projected onto me by his unfulfilled ambitions is getting whittled down by the realities of my limitations or, worse, my own interests? His blinking, uncomprehending reaction at hearing of my plans to return to Phipps as an Associate after HBS. *Playing with money? For rest of your life?* Even then, he clung to the belief that I was destined, in the great Lee tradition, to be a scholar or at least a writer. We all bear the burden of our father's expectations. For the *jangnam* in a Korean family, that burden has the weight of centuries of clan history.

The obscure warfare waged between father and son over years, a lifetime. The push of paternal expectations and the pull of desire to be your own person. The knots of father-son conflict get pulled tighter the more you tug at it. But it's not a Gordian knot you can cut with one fell stroke. No, maybe resolution does not come until the son becomes a father himself. The father-son relationship is a Möbius strip, seemingly linear and two-sided, but, at some point, somehow, it turns on itself, becomes one. The stealthy, miraculous progression of life from father to you to your son. The Möbius progression is accompanied not by complete knowledge of each other, something unattainable perhaps, but an understanding of what it means to be father and son. And an acceptance born of that understanding. The acceptance that shines down in crepuscular rays and goes deeper than expectation, broader than comprehension, straight to the throbbing heart.

"I think I understand," I tell Abuji.

Out here in the steppes, the connection between Abuji and me feels alive and true, and sufficient. The mutual acceptance, and the miracle of unspoken love that undergirds it, seems ageless, as much a part of nature as the howl of the gray wolf and the murmur of the grassland. The orange glow of the banked embers dims as we lie down to sleep our final night before returning home to America.

25

Early March 1998

The quiet in the lobby of Pyunghwa Industrial headquarters is not a peaceful quiet but an airless, stifling silence. It is not a comfort offered to visitors but a condition imposed on them for admission to a fort of official secrecy. Herein lie confidential defense contracts and clandestine operations and classified information that plumb the depths of the dark, violent human heart, privy only to those with clearance and others who would dare to know. Having arrived early at the offices of Pyunghwa (meaning "Peace"), I spend an uncomfortable half hour in the lobby atrium under the watchful eyes of two mute security guards. Abuji always said being early for an appointment is as discourteous as being late. So I wait, wordlessly in a soundless den of secrets.

When I'm brought up to the chairman's office, I am given tea and left alone in the reception annex. The room is unadorned—with just a set of low armchairs, a glass table, and two framed photographs on a wooden shelf. One photo is of President Park Chung Hee pinning a medal on a young, crisply uniformed Lieutenant Chung, the other of President Chun Doo Hwan and CEO Chung cutting a ribbon at a factory opening. Both men wear large white gloves and grasp an even larger pair of scissors, calling to mind Mickey and Minnie Mouse at Disneyland.

The chairman comes in through a side door and sits in the head armchair. He wears a tan cardigan over his shirt and tie and indoor slippers. He motions for me to drink up, doesn't say anything. He's someone comfortable in silence. Much like Abuji. Or maybe he simply enjoys other people's discomfort. I try not to fidget. Breathe, I remind myself.

Chairman Chung is called "Dragon Eyes," and I see why. He has fire in his eyes, and they bore in on me, unblinking. They're the eyes of a man who has conviction he can bend fate to his will. Once, when he found a defect in a tank belt produced in one of his factories, Dragon Eyes is said to have lined up all the supervisors and workers from the assembly line, and then he kicked them in the shins, one by one, right down the line. No faulty parts thereafter.

"I understand your father is an army man," he finally says.

"Yes, sir," I say. "For many years." I don't mention the role in intelligence or his voluntary discharge.

He's too astute to press for details. "My *dongsuh*, the deputy prime minister, tells me you did valuable service to our country. In the government financing."

"Kind of him to say, but I was just doing my job."

He nods approvingly, takes a long sip of his tea. "Lee *Yisa*, my daughter, she's very . . . special. I don't mean just that she's special to me. She is, of course. She's always been the apple of my eye. What I mean is, she's *different*."

"*Neh*." Can't disagree there.

"She grew up thinking differently, always challenging conventions. Wasn't afraid to stand up to me. You know she ran away from home during university? Got mixed up with some bad elements, student demonstrators. She stayed out on her own for two years." He shakes his head. "Mother was worried sick. But I told her Jee Yeon would be fine. My daughter is a fighter, and survivor. And I knew she'd come back home. She's her father's daughter.

"I also knew one day she'd bring home a boy who was an outsider. I thought it'd be some poor Jeolla-do boy or maybe even a foreigner." He leans in, trains his blazing eyes on mine. "I can tell you're not one of those black-haired foreigners. Am I not right?"

When I first showed up at Eagle Stone Elementary, some of my new classmates came up to me saying they wanted to touch my hair. They'd never seen jet-black hair before. I thought the strange thing was having yellow hair or brown or, strangest of all, red hair. My black hair was a marker throughout my school years, signifying my otherness. In returning to Korea, I expected to see everyone with black hair, like mine. Instead, I found brown hair, blond, red, even blue hair all around, all dyed. Chairman Chung and men of his generation are the only ones with jet-black hair, theirs dyed, too, of course.

"*Neh*," I say. I've answered a negative question in the affirmative, which means no in English but yes in Korean. I don't want to get kicked in the shins.

"She ever tell you why she left home?"

"*Anyo.*"

"Her freshman year at Ewha, she picked up somewhere that I had been involved in the 5.18 Incident." He speaks deliberately, his words measured. "Gwangju Uprising back in 1980. I'm sure you saw in Western press about the . . . what happened there. Soldiers firing on demonstrators, killing some one hundred people, though reported numbers are exaggerated. She found out I was a colonel, commanding officer of one of the paratrooper units there . . .

"Jee Yeon is so idealistic, just so naive. I suppose she knew I was protégé of General Park Chung Hee, and I got started in business thanks to support from General Chun Doo Hwan. General Chun was Military Academy 11th Class, two years my *sunbei*. He was a leader, along with later president, Roh Tae Woo, in Hanahoe, that secret group of elite officers within ROK Army that had the patronage of President Park. Hanahoe plotted to take over the country, restore order. Chun *sunbei* took me under his wing, taught me everything I know about being a leader, and a patriot."

You say Hanahoe, I say junta; but I keep the thought to myself.

"In 1979, 12.12, following the death of President Park, then General Chun and his Hanahoe cohorts succeeded in a coup d'état. As de facto leader of country, General Chun declared martial law. We needed stability in our country at that time." Like many life-long army men, Jee Yeon's father evinces a sacred belief in the military as a moral authority, a *necessary* force in a disorderly, dissolute society. "Well, the students and citizens of Gwangju disagreed. They wanted freedom immediately. They were like children wanting their candy. General Chun decreed: order first, then freedom. Starting in April 1980, people started staging protests." He closes his eyes.

I sense where this is headed, and my stomach clenches.

"At first, they were peaceful," he says. "We let them do their childish venting. Demanding an end to martial law, and free speech, democratic elections, everything—right away. Then the protests spread, they got unruly. Daily skirmishes with local police. In mid-May, a student from Jeonnam University lit himself on fire, to protest US President Reagan's support of Chun's autocratic rule. Protest US support!" He opens his fiery eyes again. "Did this ingrate not realize where we'd be today without US intervention in 6.25 War? We'd all be eating gruel in unified Communist Korea!" He shakes his head.

The grainy photo comes back to me, a thin man burning himself alive in the middle of a thoroughfare in Gwangju. He remained sitting in a lotus position as flames swallowed his body.

"The student's self-immolation lit the fuse. Protests just spiraled out of control. On May 18, about two hundred students who'd gathered at Jeonnam University overpowered thirty riot policemen. Protesters gathered a few hundred more people, and the mob marched on downtown Gwangju. It was then I was sent down there by Major General Chun to suppress the revolt. That's what it was, a revolt. Threatened to undo everything we'd worked so hard to make. I was one of the two commanders of 680 paratroopers from the 33rd and 35th battalions of the 7th Airborne Brigade. We got intelligence there were radical elements, Communist sympathizers, including one Kim Dae Jung, among the organizers. They were a threat to order."

One man's revolt, I think, is another man's democratization movement.

"We were there as a show of force, to deter further rioting. But when the mob saw real soldiers, they started throwing stones and Molotov cocktails at us. A few men under my command caught on fire. You ever smell burning flesh?"

"*Anyo,*" I say.

"We held the line until the 20th. That day, a huge, unruly mob gathered in front of Gwangju Station. They'd looted a police armory nearby, and many of them had M1 rifles and carbines. And, remember, these were not kids but dangerous people with training from their military service."

"They shot first?"

"It was chaos. To this day, I don't know who fired the first shots. But I can tell you, contrary to later reports, I did not get any official order from Major General Chun to shoot at the citizens. I did not order the shooting . . . Tear gas, yes, but not live rounds."

"But someone did."

"Lee *Yisa*, you've never been in battle. A battlefield is chaos. That's what it was that day. There were shots, I don't know from which side first, but my paratroopers did what they were trained to do. They overwhelmed the enemy with force."

The enemy? "But they were innocent civilians," I say, trying to control my voice. "Some six hundred of them got killed—"

He turns his dragon eyes on me. "Son, there were no innocent people that day."

"I read the soldiers used bayonets on the people. I heard they were crazed from amphetamines and steroids the army fed them—"

"Don't believe everything you read in the papers. We did what we had to do to protect our country. They grew into a militia, and it took us six days to suppress them, and restore order in Gwangju." He sighs. "Dark chapter in our history. But a soldier does his duty."

I remember the look on Abuji's face when he heard the news of the Gwangju Massacre back when I was in junior high school. A look of black horror. "The curse on the country has finally come home," he said. Soldiers killing our own people. He tried to hide the news photos. But I saw them. Men and women in civilian clothes getting clubbed, blood dripping down their faces, young men getting dragged by their hair by soldiers wearing gas masks, bloodstained corpses lining the streets. A wailing woman, carrying the limp body of a small boy in her arms.

"For shame, for shame," Abuji kept saying. "Not even Kim Il Sung in North does this." He condemned General Chun as "the Butcher of Gwangju."

Abuji drank that evening. I can still hear the clink of the ice cubes in his glass of Chivas and see his tobacco-stained fingers as he smoked Marlboros all night. He said, "Today, I am ashamed to be Korean." Words I thought I'd never hear from Abuji's mouth.

"That's why Jee Yeon left home," Chairman Chung says. "She held me to blame for the atrocities in Gwangju. I had someone keep tabs on her, of course. Just to make sure she was all right, stayed out of big trouble. I knew she'd come back. She'd left her cello behind.

"And I have to give her credit—she never once came home to beg for money. Tough little cookie. Wish her brother had her toughness."

Parents don't choose their children, any more than we choose our parents. Their choice is in accepting who we are.

"My *ttal*, she has a good heart. She just needs the right man." He reaches over, puts a heavy hand on my thigh. "Lee *Yisa*, I know you'll take care of her." It's an order, not a request.

"I'll do my best, sir," I say. As if his daughter needed taking care of, this woman who found the music in her soul despite the dark secrets in her father's past.

26

Mid-March 1998

As we enter the Ilsung Motors factory grounds in Changwon, we see smoke billowing out of the two tall chimneys that stand like minarets above the industrial complex. Jack and I have come to Changwon on a site visit as part of our seller due diligence—though I have my own reasons. The front gate is chained; behind it, a crowd, men with red bandannas around their heads, shouting in unison. We identify ourselves as "consultants," and, after some checking, they let us through.

"Come one, come all," Jack says. "Step right up and enjoy the show. Behold the wondrous acts inside the Ilsung circus tent."

Inside the compound, we see the smoke is not from the chimneys. Someone has set fire to a container, its steel exterior melting like a wilting flower as it sends spirals of thick black smoke skyward. A helicopter whirs through the smoke. We pass the demonstrators seated on the ground in rows, chanting, fists pumping in rhythm. Many of them have ski goggles on their foreheads. There is debris all around, and the ground below them is uneven, rolling, as in a Hundertwasser structure. I can taste burned metal on my tongue, and it makes me queasy.

The cheer has been wiped off Jack's face. "Maybe we should come back another day," he says.

"We're here," I say. "Let's do our diligence." I tell him to go find the CFO's office, where we're expected, and I'll join him shortly.

I cross the compound in search of the paint and finish factory building. There is a fence along the perimeter, and on the other side I see green vinyl tents with hand-painted signs, HOPE TENTS. The women there are middle-aged and some elderly, leaning on canes, and their wailing has an undulating rhythm of its own. They wave handkerchiefs at their husbands and sons inside the compound. Their tear-soaked handkerchiefs barely flutter in the wind. Some hold up posters that read, WE ARE WITH YOU and COME BACK SAFELY. As I walk by, a couple of women, sobbing, plead with me to take some *kimbap* and bottled water to their husbands. One woman asks me to bring her son some Choco Pies. The sight of the distinctive brown-and-red wrappers stops me in my tracks. The chocolate snacks of my childhood. My madeleines.

When I was six, I limped home to Umma after skinning my knee from a bicycle fall. She brought out the red bottle of *Aka-jinki*, and I ran away. She coaxed me back with the promise of a

Choco Pie. Umma applied the iodine tincture with a Q-tip, leaving an orange areola, and blew on it. Then she gave me, as a reward for being such a brave boy, a Choco Pie. The exquisite pleasure of my first bite of the chocolate-marshmallow sponge overwhelmed the senses. Licking the gooey chocolate off my fingers made me forget all about the sting. From then on, whenever something bad happened to me, Umma would give me the chocolate treat. When I got a polio inoculation or didn't get invited to a friend's birthday party, when Appa left for America, she was there with a Choco Pie. She said every bad thing that happened could be offset by a bite of Choco Pie.

I take the boxes of Choco Pie. Someone from a Hope Tent releases a plastic bag of light green balloons, which float jauntily skyward—a postcard of hope ascendant—before being swallowed up in the black smoke.

I find the paint building, thanks to a huge banner with bloodred letters hanging from the roof: LAYOFF IS MURDER! The labor union has taken over the top floor. Union men stand on the roof wearing hard hats and holding long steel pipes, and their clang reverberates to the ground floor. I can feel the electricity crackling among them, as a fuse about to get lit. I walk up five flights of stairs to their main office.

"Yoon *buweewonjang-nim*?" I say, knocking on an open door. "Yoon Jung Ha-*ssi*?"

A man glares up from a small group gathered at a desk. He's in his midthirties, the lines creasing his forehead belying his age. Behind the wire-rim glasses, there are soft eyes and a baby's mouth, the kind of face that saw love from his family and joy in his youth. A life of daily breakfasts, *dwenjang guk, ghim,* and rice, some fried eggs, enjoyed with his family. But that's long in the past. No shave or haircut, or a laugh, I'd guess, in a long time. Just a trace of white toothpaste under his nostrils, a balm for the tear gas, I learn.

Yoon is about to ask who I am, then he sees the Choco Pie box under my arm and the leather briefcase I'm holding. "Ah, Jee Yeon's friend," he says. He's neither polite nor rude. "You picked a hell of a day to visit. Wait for me outside."

When he comes out to see me, Yoon drags his Prospecs sneakers like slippers, his heels over the accordioned backs. He doesn't bother with pleasantries. "We began our strike a week ago," he says. "Militants from Daehan NoChong are pushing for all-out war. They say it's the only way to get on the news, grab the public's attention. I'm seeking a more peaceable compromise. Bring management to the table for discussion. Forget wage hikes. We know these are difficult times. Just job security. No layoffs. Maybe get some union representation on the board of directors, as they do in German companies."

He wipes the sweat off his forehead. "Jee Yeon tells me you're with Phipps, the bank that's helping to sell off the company. Are you part of that team?"

"I am."

He sighs bitterly. "Do you have any idea what foreigners will do with this company? They'll cut the workforce in half. At least. That's three thousand men—three thousand families. And it's already started ..."

I look down.

"You're an educated guy. They ever make you read John Locke? When a company hires a man, that company enters into a moral pact. If he works hard, they take care of him. Firing workers at will is a violation of that sacred pact. We used to have lifetime employment in our country. But Korean companies and management have learned from the Americans. Now we have layoffs, too. 'Restructuring,' they call it. The difference is, in the US, over half the workers get a new job within six months. In Korea, it's close to zero. That's the job market, yes, but it's also the culture, the stigma. You get laid off, it means you must not have worked hard enough. The men are ostracized, their families get broken up . . .'"

"Yes, I realize—"

"That's what this work stoppage is about. It's a preemptive protest. Sell us irresponsibly to a foreign operator, and you won't have *any* workforce. No workers, no company. So promise us no layoffs."

"Is it working?" I say. "The strike?"

He has a pained expression. "We're playing right into management's hands. They ordered us back to work, knowing we wouldn't go back. That gave them the excuse to bring on the riot police. You ever been shot with a water cannon?"

I can't say that I have.

"They shoot it at your face, you feel like you're drowning. Shoot it at your body, knocks you off your feet, leaves bruises on your torso for days. Not as bad as tear gas, though. You see those helicopters hovering above us? They're equipped with lique-fied tear gas, much more 'effective' than regular gas. That's what

217

they're threatening us with. And this morning, they turned off our water.

"But I'll tell you what's worse. The tension between the guys laid off and the ones spared, who're still working. Guilt, and anger and recrimination. The spared ones think, 'There but for the grace of God.' The others think, 'Why me?' Management turns them against each other. We've seen confrontations. It's taking a heavy psychological toll."

He grimaces, as though from physical pain. "Last week, a worker, one of the spared ones . . . he committed suicide. He just couldn't take the guilt, and the pressure."

He lets this sink in, and we're silent for a while.

"How'd you end up . . . here?" I ask, just to say something.

"This is where they keep the paint. We have over two hundred thousand liters of flammable material. They wouldn't dare attack us here."

Seeing the look on my face, he says, "I want a peaceful resolution. But I'm no Gandhi."

"I meant how did you end up leading the union?"

Yoon takes off his glasses, wipes the lenses with his shirt-front. "I woke up this morning with one thought: today's the day I make these people's lives better. Tonight I'll go to sleep, and in the morning, I'll have one thought, Today I will make these people's lives better. One goal in my life. Only thing that matters."

He looks at me, his soft eyes turning firm. "You can make their lives better."

I know better than to speak.

"You know what I'm talking about," he says. "Your project—"

Just then we hear a loud bang, then a deafening roar outside. Yoon and I run to the window. A battle has broken out on the factory grounds.

Yoon gasps, cries out, "No, no, *no!*" as he brushes past me and out the door.

Below, on one side are the striking workers, all wearing white masks with goggles pulled over them. They attack, armed with stones and slingshots full of nails, then they retreat and attack again. From the far side, a force of riot police and private thugs marches in military formation, wielding full-body shields and billy clubs. They press forward, and SWAT teams flanking them pick off protesters, throw them in trucks.

Helicopters spray streams of what looks like water but I gather, from its effects on the people below, is liquid CS gas. The workers are disoriented but throb with the desperate energy of a cornered animal. They lob green soju bottles with fiery rag tails as they retreat. A banner behind them reading, WE STAND READY TO DIE FOR OUR CAUSE, hangs crooked, half-torn.

I see a riot policeman get hit flush with a Molotov cocktail, his back and arms catching on fire. The flames shoot up, engulf him. He throws himself off the top of a SWAT truck and rolls on the ground as his colleagues stomp his back with their boots. Tendrils of smoke rise off his still body.

As soon as I step outside, my eyes start burning. Now I understand what the ski goggles were for. The tear gas assaults all my senses at once, and for a minute, I'm sure my eyes are bleeding and I'm going blind. I am become King Lear. Or more like the Duke of Gloucester, eyes ripped out. For some reason, I can't hear, either. The roar of the crowd has become a dull reverberation. I cough violently. My nose runs. I can't see, can't hear. I can't breathe.

I'm enveloped in fog, a mix of smoke and tear gas and dirt kicked up by the fighting mob. For a moment, I am suspended in time, alone, in a vacuum of noise and bodies. The chaos around me recedes. There's a long bamboo stick on the ground in front of me, left there like a gift. It feels right in my hand, the grip, the weight distribution, the supple hardness. The noise returns, and I fall in behind some protesters. I start swinging my stick like a baseball bat, though I can't see well. I hit somebody in front of me, I'm pretty sure a policeman, with a satisfying *thwack* on his shoulder.

A figure emerges from the fog. My eyes clear just enough for me to make out his SWAT uniform and a black helmet that glistens in a dagger of sunlight. He points his billy club at me, and I croak, "Darth Vader," just before he drives his baton into my gut, knocking the breath out of me. I try to summon some old tae kwon do moves, but my legs won't move. Another SWAT guy appears out of nowhere, knocks the stick out of my hand, and sweeps my feet from under me in a clean judo swipe. I fall facedown on the ground. I taste the coppery dirt.

There's the sound of a thick crack, and a body, a protester, falls down next to me. He's been clubbed in the head, and a trickle of blood rolls down his forehead and into his goggles, where it forms a small red puddle. One of the SWAT guys plants a knee on my back. He spits, "*Ppalgengyi,*" in my ear.

Dirty Communist. With the full weight of his body on me, I'm suffocating.

Jack comes to my rescue. "Hey, hey, officer, sir," he tells them, his palms up. "Just a case of mistaken identity. He's not who you think he is. This guy's with me, not one of them." He helps me gingerly to my feet.

I protest, say I *am* one of them. But they either don't hear or choose to ignore me. They release me with a dismissive shove. I turn back to look for the man with the head wound, but Jack yanks me away. "Hey, easy there, cowboy."

When we're at a safe distance from the action, he says, "You okay? For Chrissake, you could've been killed out there."

"I'm fine," I say.

"Let's get the hell out of here." Jack leads me by the elbow.

I look around for my box of Choco Pies.

"Lose your briefcase?" he says.

"No. Yes. I mean, doesn't matter. Don't need it anymore."

As we hurry past the front gate, I see behind us the blackened carcass of a torched Ilsung Motors sedan in the middle of the factory yard. Dark fumes swirl from it. The roar of the mob dissipates with the smoke from the factory.

"A fucking war zone," Jack says, shaking his head.

I take a bottle of water from him, pour cool water in my stinging eyes.

"Listen, little buddy. Word gets out about this union shitshow, no one's gonna touch T-ball. I think we should get to Daimler pronto and proactively—"

"Tell them what?" I say. "That they're gonna buy a workforce of happy campers?"

"That we'll agree to an asset sale. Forget the debt—leave it behind. Forget the contingent liabilities, for that matter. Just take what you want."

"Yeah? How about the workers? Forget their job security, too?"

He sighs. "What I'm saying is, it behooves us to be reasonable here, for the firm. Under the circumstances."

"'It behooves us, for the firm . . . ?"

"Yeah, you remember, the guys who sign your paycheck every month? And give you a nice, fat bonus at year-end?"

"Under the circumstances," I repeat. "I suppose it would *behoove* us to be reasonable in price, too."

"We'll signal we'll be . . . yeah, realistic in price, too. Fuck, all right, cheap."

"Priced to go."

"Fuckin' A, to go! Price goes down, we . . . we'll still get our guaranteed minimum fee, right?"

I look at him.

"Right?"

I can barely see out of my still-tearing eyes.

"Christ, you look like hell," he says. "Your eyes, all red, full of pus. Can you see?"

"Yeah, fine," I tell him. "I can see now."

27

Mid-March 1998

After Changwon, I can't talk to anyone. How can anyone understand the jumble of emotions I'm feeling, the anger and frustration and guilt? I keep to myself at work, doing only what I have to, and avoid colleagues, even Jun. When I call Jee Yeon to finalize our dinner plans, I realize they're the first full sentences I've exchanged with someone in two days.

We meet after work at Tongin Sijang, a traditional street market not far from my office in the Hanguk Life Building. I wanted to take her to a proper restaurant for our first real date, but when I asked her what she wanted to eat, Japanese, French, Italian, she said whatever you like, Dae Joon-*ssi*. I said *ttukbokki*, the spicy rice cakes of my childhood. She laughed, said she knew just the place.

The *sijang* is in an alleyway tucked behind skyscrapers in the central business district, a juxtaposition of the traditional with the modern that people say gives Seoul its charm. We walk down the serpentine alley, hemmed in by stalls selling dried pollack hung on a line like laundry, dried seaweed and anchovies on our left, *makgulli*, dried persimmon, fresh tangerines, and *hallabong* on our right. The brine of the sea mixes with the citrus of Jeju to produce a tangy sulfuric smell that is insistently local. The curly-permed *ajummas* manning the stalls, unrepentantly unmodernized in garb and manner, complete the local effect.

As we walk, I ask Jee Yeon, as casually as possible, if I passed the test with ol' Dragon Eyes. She just smiles, pulls my arm around her shoulders.

We arrive at the famous *ttukbokki* stand, where there is not a stand, just two white plastic stools. My stool squeaks when I sit, forces me to concentrate on keeping my balance. The owner-chef, *Imo* to everyone, uses thick, swollen hands to stir the red rice cakes in a scarred black wok to get them good and sticky. Jee Yeon explains the *ttukbokki* here is special because it's wok-fried, not braised, and, well, it's pretty spicy.

I take her warning as a personal challenge, and I put a heaping chopsticksful in my mouth. The *ttuk* sizzles on my tongue, and the taste is overwhelmed by the sensation of endorphins firing from the sharp pain. "Just as I remember it," I say, my eyes watering. I wonder out loud if they eat *ttukbokki* in North Korea.

Jee Yeon, grown accustomed to my wayward musings, says, not missing a beat, "Probably. After all, *mandoo*, dumplings, are from the North, and they put *ttuk* in their *mandooguk*."

"You think Korea will ever be reunified?" I say.

"I used to think so, sometime in my lifetime. Now . . ."

Abuji taught me not to talk politics on dates. "Don't you think Koreans should laugh more?" I say.

"I don't think laughter equals happiness. Happiness is something attained. Not manufactured."

We finish our *ttukbokki* in silence.

She notices the splint I have on my right forefinger, lifts it to examine. "Does it hurt?"

Not as much as my pride. Or my conscience. Shaking my head, I say, "I'm not sure where I hurt it. At the factory somewhere. I met your old *sunbei*, the union guy."

She nods.

"I can't get the ringing of their chants out of my ears. The protesting laborers . . ."

She listens, as good listeners do, without judging.

"You should've seen it . . . the tear gas, the smoke, the beatings, the blood . . ." I can barely get the words out. "It was . . . obscene."

Jee Yeon falls into a deep quiet. "You know, in my student days, when I was doing all those protest marches, I saw it all . . . the hate, the violence."

My turn to be the listener, she the confider.

"But we kept at it." She lights a cigarette. "Because we believed in what we were fighting for. Changing society . . . It drove Appa crazy. Not just because it was against his politics, but we were demonstrating against his Military Academy *sunbei*, President Chun. He took it personally."

"Parents always take it personally."

"He never said so, but I think he wanted me to join the company, get groomed in the family business. He thought I had a better head for business than Oppa. But Umma would never allow it. She thinks good girls from good families should play music and get married right out of Ewha. That's what she did."

"So you rebelled."

"I followed my heart. You know about the June Uprising of '87? I participated in the sit-ins, the marches. It was beautiful, true, something we believed in. The demonstration at Yonsei, June 9th, when that student Lee Han Yeol was critically wounded by a tear gas grenade, I was there. You must've seen the photo, Han Yeol in his Yonsei T-shirt, unconscious, blood trickling down his forehead as he's dragged off by another demonstrator. It started out as a peaceful sit-in, we sang Yang Hee Eun songs all afternoon. You know the lyrics to "Morning Dew"?

After the long night, on every leaf,
Like morning dew prettier than pearls,
The sorrow in my bosom forms in drops,
As the sun rises red over the cemetery.

"Pretty, sad," I say.

"We were singing, and then the riot police showed up and, without warning, started firing tear gas at us. Probably tear gas produced by Appa's company. All hell broke loose. We thought it was gonna turn into another Gwangju Massacre."

"Yet you, the students prevailed." I remember the pictures of long-haired students triumphantly waving *Taegukgi*, the Korean flag, in the streets.

"Lee Han Yeol died in the hospital. We had a martyr. It helped, of course, that he was photogenic, in the flower of youth, and from a SKY school. His name became a rallying cry for the democracy movement. The whole country, laborers, religious groups, taxi drivers, even salarymen, rose up. All of Korea took to the streets, millions marching, demanding freedom.

"Dictator Chun finally succumbed. His handpicked successor, General Roh Tae Woo, issued the June 29 Democratic Declaration, calling for free, direct elections and releasing dissident Kim Dae Jung. We broke the long, uninterrupted line of dictators, Park Chung Hee to Chun Doo Hwan to Roh Tae Woo."

"Boy, you and my *abuji* would have a lot to talk about."

"I'd like to meet him. . . I feel like I know him already from all your stories."

"Soon, I hope." Before it's too late.

"That was the start of real democracy in our country," she says. "There were mass celebrations in the streets. I just broke down and cried. You know what it feels like to get something you fought for with your soul, risking jail and worse?"

I admit I do not.

"But that was it. We had our moment. After the June Uprising, I couldn't deal with the violence anymore, all the anger and the hate. And the grubby politics. We got our democracy. I just didn't feel it anymore. Is it strange that I missed my cello?"

"Not at all. You are a musician. That's what you are. In addition to bomb thrower." A bomb thrower from inside the palace, the most courageous kind.

She gives one of her soft laughs. "Ironic, no? The daughter of a bomb maker throwing bombs? And getting teargassed for it?" A long puff. "Feels like a long time ago. I still have dreams about those days. Bad nightmares. Of the riot police." Another long puff. "I hope it wasn't all in vain. That hard-won democracy . . . I pray we didn't fight to gain our political freedom only to subject the people to economic tyranny."

"The chaebol . . ."

"Chaebol oligarchs," she says. "Yesterday's dictators have been replaced by industrial oligarchs today. A handful of chaebol, people like my *appa* but worse, control Korean society, the economy, media, politics, education—all of it through their tentacles of corruption. And isn't it a worse kind of oppression, more insidious, because the people—"

"They're not aware of it," I add. "Engels's 'false consciousness.' They live in the system, perpetuate it, in the name of prosperity."

"Unless someone does something about it," she says, turning to look at me. "Fight for 'economic democratization,' so people may have economic freedom."

"Change is coming," I say. "One deal, one company at a time."

"I knew there was a fighter in you," she says, "the first time we met." She squeezes my hand.

Buddhists in the Goguryeo Dynasty believed in a human-like bird called *Inmyeonjo* that connected the sky and earth. Legend had it that only those with a pure heart could hear the bird's song, the most beautiful voice in the heavens. I believe I can hear Jee Yeon's voice, and it's beautiful.

"That makes one of us," I say. Maybe returning home is regaining purity in your heart. "Still not sure."

Jee Yeon puts out her stub. "Filthy habit," she says. "Picked it up in those days."

"I don't mind the smell of cigarettes," I say.

It's a reminder, for her and for me, of a time past.

Love isn't declared in Korean; it's *confessed*, a *kobak*. As if love were a secret, to be kept hidden away until the right time. Then, and only then, do you let it out of the bag, confide your most personal story.

"I need to go to New Jersey," I confide to her. "I'll be back in a week. Maybe we can go for that reading then? Our *koonghap*."

She nods, agrees it's time.

28

I have a recurring dream. I'm in Sinchon, in the old part of Seoul, trying to find our old home. The small house built of red brick, with a dirt yard out front and the lone persimmon tree. I walk alone, and I know I know the way home. I cross a grove, now bare, with only a few well-trodden patches of brown-green, our old playing field where we used to kick around a soccer ball, then up a rolling hill. My feet follow the familiar topography. There's a woman, a vaguely familiar face, with a baby strapped to her back. At the bottom of the hill, I come to a cluster of cottages.

There are children, laughing and yelling, though their sound is muffled, chasing a small three-wheeled truck spraying disinfectant down the street. The truck billows contrails of white smoke, and the children dance deliriously in the fog, just as we used to.

I make my way down an alleyway, brushing the cool concrete walls with my fingers. It's such a familiar feel. I know from memory it's a left, then a right. I pass houses I recognize. But when I make the turns, there are only more alleyways. The alleys are deserted. I go through what becomes a maze, turning left, and right, then randomly right and left. I start panicking, and I start running. But the faster I run, the more lost I get. I run out of breath. I cry out, but no one can hear me.

Finally, I come to the end of an alley that looks familiar and where I know our home should be. It's a dead end. I look left and right. No persimmon tree. There is only a forbidding gate of two bronze doors with intricate carvings.

As I get closer, I can make out dozens of figures on what look like Rodin's *The Gates of Hell*. The figures move, and they're in varying stages of agony. Women writhe in pain, couples tear at each other's faces, a man eats an infant. In the middle, a lone man sits, naked, still, contemplating the anguish and suffering around him.

I back away and look behind me and around. Home is nowhere in sight, lost to me forever.

29

Mid–late March 1998

The house in Fort Lee looks the same, but my memory moves over it like a great octopus, tentacles exploring every room, feeling about the front yard, trying to suck dried meaning out of every nook and space. My old room, where I first heard whispers of my destiny and charted my initial awkward steps out into the world. The cupboards in the kitchen where Dongseng would hide Abuji's packs of Marlboros, always to be discovered. The swing set out back, where little Dongseng used to catapult high into the sky. The shrubbery around the side where I got stung by a bee and, in family lore, cried out, "It burns! It burns!" Our front yard, whence my mighty yellow stick sent Wiffle balls whistling over the fence, propelling Appa down the hill in panting pursuit to retrieve the missiles. The shriveled persimmon tree, a souvenir of our past life.

All from a time when the world outside seemed impossibly huge, rumbling with obscure promise and magical, astonishing things to unfold before me. There was deep meaning to it all to be unfurled, I was sure, as from an ancient scroll. And my *appa* a giant astride the house, steeped in wisdom and possessing the power to impose some order on a baffling, mysterious world.

Abuji has come back to the house from a month in the hospital. He's returned a shrunken, fainter version of himself, one I barely recognize. Gone is the vividness, the coiled strength, the *music*. He lies in bed all day, tethered to a respirator. He mumbles and moans in his sleep, and when he's awake, for brief stretches, his labored breathing allows just a few words from his always dry mouth. He has a tear lodged in the corner of his eyes, refusing yet to drop.

Rage, I want desperately to tell him: *rage against the dying of the light. Do not go gentle into that good night*. Go on fighting it. As you always taught me. We'll fight together.

But in my heart I know it's too late. The time to fight is over, behind my frail *abuji*. You can see it in his slumping form on the bed. Umma already knows. All we can ask for now is peace.

I sit by the bed, hold his hand. I give him a shave, trim his week-old white stubble. He touches a fragile finger to my cheek. When he's feeling better, I sit him up and feed him some chocolate Ensure through a straw. Dongseng comes in and out of the room, checking on the oxygen level, feeding him *jook*, porridge with bits of abalone.

Umma keeps us company, tells us stories. Old tales of ghosts and spells and curses. Some dusted-off stories about our childhood,

Abuji's favorites. Abuji listens when he's awake, sometimes smiles a distant smile in remembrance. She retells the story of my *dol*, the first anniversary of birth, the traditional rite of beginning life.

"Nineteen sixty-eight, January twenty-first," she says, her eyes coming alive. "All the relatives and friends gathered for your celebration . . . the same day the North Korean commandos came down and raided the Blue House. Can you imagine? Nearly succeeded in killing President Park Chung Hee."

Abuji interrupts to say, between breaths, "That Kim Il Sung, even crazier than the Dictator." He fills his lungs with pumped oxygen. "They deserve each other."

"We had all this food, several different kinds of *ttuk*. And everyone was just glued to TV," Umma continues. "When the TV broadcast cut off, we listened to radio. We weren't sure the president had survived. We thought, maybe beginning of another invasion from the North."

I remember Abuji first telling me the story when I was in elementary school. The special ops commandos from North Korea, thirty-one from the famed Unit 124, all handpicked by Kim Il Sung. They had been selected in their teens for their physical toughness, intelligence, and dedication to the Eternal Leader. Legend had it that the group started with over fifty soldiers, but nineteen were killed in a survival-of-the-fittest hand combat among themselves. The commandos' mission, crisply articulated afterward by the lone captive, Kim Shin-Jo: "To cut the throat of Traitor Park."

The group crossed the border to the South under cover of night and trekked forty-eight kilometers on foot, running with thirty-kilogram gear over mountainous terrain. Disguised in ROK Army uniforms, they got past the heavily fortified militarized zone. But thirty-six hours into their trip, they ran into four men from a farming village. The Li brothers were out cutting wood. The commandos debated killing them but made the fateful decision to give them an ideological indoctrination on Communism and then release them. The Lis immediately raised the alarm; the hunt was on.

An entire ROK Army division was unleashed on a manhunt across mountains and villages. But the superhuman commandos eluded them, outpacing the dragnet at every checkpoint. The assassins made it to the backyard of the Blue House. There they engaged in a furious firefight with the security forces. The North Koreans were wiped out; two who were about to be captured slit their own throats. Only one survived to tell the tale.

"That's how we celebrated your *dol*," Umma says.

"You began life with a bang," Abuji adds.

When Abuji told me this story, the North Korean commandos secretly captured my imagination for their audacity, even as he condemned them as the misguided foot soldiers of a Communist madman. They must have known they were going on a suicide mission, and yet they carried it out, roaring with white-hot fury.

Umma leaves, and I'm alone with Abuji. I tell him about Project Thunderball. I'm not sure how much registers. "Getting Thunderball done would hurt the workers. But not doing it would mean turning my back on my friend Wayne, who entrusted this big project to me. Damned if I do, damned if I don't."

Abuji is quiet. I think he's drifted off again, when he mutters, barely audibly, "What will happen . . . to workers?"

"Some of them, probably many of them, will be restructured."

He stares blankly at me.

"Laid off. Many will be laid off."

He closes his eyes.

"Jee Yeon put me in touch with the labor leader, someone she knew. She thought I should hear from the workers' side . . . so I can get the full picture."

"Wise girl," he says. He inhales through the tubes. "You remember . . . story of . . . the peasant with the butterflies?"

"The one about the man who could make butterflies out of thin air? Think you said Halabuji told you the story? You told it to me when I was little."

He nods.

"How's it go?" I reach back in my memory for the details. "There was a quiet, plain man, with no discernible gifts, but he'd take threads of silk in different colors, put them in his palm. And then he'd blow on it? No, he'd say a chant or something, and then when he'd open his hand, butterflies would fly out, float all around in the air."

"Beautiful butterflies . . . dazzling in their many colors."

In Abuji's telling, the butterflies were always beautiful, dazzling. "Right, blue butterflies, and yellow and red and orange. How was he able to do that again?" I say. "By some magic?"

"Taoists call it *son-sul* . . . They believe there are . . . invisible elements in the air, which can be controlled and summoned to be manifested . . . in various forms of life . . . foxes, birds, butterflies. By some people."

"Which people?"

"People whose insides are light . . . so it's same weight as air around you . . . By having an emptied conscience."

By doing the right thing.

He gives me a wan smile, taps my hand. "My *adeul* . . ."

What will I do when my *abuji* is not around to give me advice? Who knows me well enough and cares about me enough to tell me what I need to hear, to feel? Whom will I turn to for wisdom, and butterflies?

I hold my father's thin hand until he falls asleep, then go downstairs.

Warm, familiar odors of Lemon-Gladed furniture and ripened kimchi greet me. The sweet-pungent smell of my past, my *otherness*, I'd tried so hard to leave behind in my schooldays. Old framed family photos sit on the mantel bearing still the image of false settledness.

Pings from piano keys come from the family room. Donseng sits at the piano, where Abuji used to play Chopin, Mozart, Liszt. The black Yamaha has chipped corners, vestiges of wayward swings of my baseball bat.

"Appa taught me to play on this piano," she says. "We played 'Chopsticks' on it. It's so out of tune now. Hasn't been played in years." She breaks down in tears, buries her face in her hands. Her shoulders heave, and, unable to find words of comfort, I just put my hand on her shoulder.

Umma is in the kitchen, sitting at the breakfast table. A thick book is open in front of her.

"He's resting," I tell her.

She notices me looking at the book, a textbook titled *Major Works in American Literature*. "Studying for class," she says, with a tired smile. "Test next week. Much harder than I remember it."

"Class?" I say. "Test?"

"I've been going to school. Montclair State, studying English. Your father, he enrolled me there last term."

Umma's taking college classes?

"He wanted me to speak English well. Prepare me for life on my own, after he . . ." She can't finish the sentence. With some effort, she tucks a wisp of gray hair behind her ear.

Just like Abuji, to plan, and prepare her. To make sure she could survive on her own, as a widow. My insides feel hollowed out.

"We'll be around," I say. "We'll both help you manage."

"You're busy with your life. And your little sister, she's just getting started at the law firm." She takes my hand, holds it in hers. "Adeul, when will you settle down? Abuji and I, we've waited so long for you to meet a good girl, from a good family. Someone like Jee Yeon. Are you making plans, to start your own family?" She doesn't say, before it's too late for your father.

"I will, Umma," I say. "Soon. I promise." Then I excuse myself for a conference call. Business, important, I tell her.

*

As I go into the study, Abuji's private sanctuary, I'm again the boy sneaking into his father's forbidden sanctum sanctorum in Seoul. The awe of entering sacred space mingled with the thrill of trespassing. The mahogany shelves overflow with books, some stacked in piles. There are the books from his study back in Seoul, his classics of Western literature and history and philosophy. His prized calf leather–bound volumes of Shakespeare's First Folio, spines crumbling, pages yellowed, but still full of beauty and sound and fury. There are more Korean authors than I remember. Yoon Dong Joo, Park Kyung Li, Hwang Suk Young, Cho Jung Rae. As though after a lifetime of reading Western works in Korea, now, in America, he's gone back to Korean literature. In the center of the room, a lone wooden Nakashima Conoid chair. Abuji's reading chair, where he would sit for hours and read the wisdom of the universe.

I feel like I'm committing a sacrilege doing business in this temple. But duty calls. I need to conjure butterflies.

The Daimler-Benz Corporate Strategy people have asked for a call on Thunderball on short notice. Just when Jack and I were debating reaching out to them. In every deal, there comes a point when the art of M&A, what practitioners call tactics, trumps the science. You spend weeks, sometimes months, on quantitative analysis, parsing data, running financial models to arrive at a valuation, only to throw it out the window in favor of the "intangibles," a fancy word for emotion and ego. And you justify the extra in price in the holy name of synergies from the combined operations. The art hinges on points of leverage—who has it in negotiations and when—and the leverage in the early part of a sale process is with the seller. This is when the buyer's greed ("I want this accretive asset bad") and fear ("Holy shit, I'm going to lose it to my competitor") are at their peak. By asking for a call, Daimler has signaled its greed and fear.

When I gave the head of our M&A Department a heads-up, Conway mistook it for a consultation and fed me all sorts of advice. He quoted Machiavelli: "War is never avoided; it is only postponed to someone's advantage." He cited Sun Tzu: "Know thyself, know thy enemy. The supreme art of war is to subdue the enemy without fighting." If Mammon is the god worshipped on Wall Street, Sun Tzu and Machiavelli are the apostles. And Tony Montana, with his little friend. They are quoted as scripture, the lines from *Scarface* with particular relish. "Remember," Conway said, "your job is to make a wedding, not a funeral," mixing metaphors and commingling clichés.

I told Jack I'd take this conference call alone, and he skipped a beat before saying, Okay. His parting words of wisdom: "Just don't fuck it up, Shane." Wayne's reaction to the scheduling of the call was "Got 'em right where we want 'em!"

The Daimler people have a reputation as strategic acquirers with pricing discipline. They don't use bankers or advisers—they don't need to. I expect a fishing expedition by them and, if they sense weakness, possibly a lowball first offer.

The Germans are, true to form, serious and direct. Their point man, a VP named Dr. Johannes Hesse—all German bankers I know have doctorates—gets on with a terse hello. He likes to be called Dr. Hesse.

"Hello, Johannes," I say. I wait, let him start the discussion.

Hesse says, in clipped English, "We called to say we are potentially interested on a preliminary, indicative, nonbinding basis, but only at the right price and conditions."

"We welcome your interest," I say. "But, as you know, we're running a process. With multiple interested parties." Join the party of one.

"We prefer to have bilateral discussions," he says. His words come out like marching soldiers. "Not participate in a competitive auction."

"Your preference is noted," I say, cool as *bingsoo*. Bilateral meaning exclusivity in negotiations. It's the tipping point in any deal process: when a buyer gets it, the power in negotiations shifts to them. The less I say at this point, the better. Information is the valuable commodity, and, as seller adviser, I have it, they don't. A good M&A tactician levers the information asymmetry to maximum advantage. I need to hoard the information on which options we have and what we might do; given my motives, moreover, I need to make a show of hoarding it.

Silence on the other end. I can picture them discussing among themselves, with their phone on mute. They've tested us, to see how desperate a seller we are; I've responded, not so much. As is my habit on conference calls, I doodle, covering a sheet of yellow legal paper with butterflies and some notes.

"What we mean is," Hesse says, sounding less sure, "our management has a long history with the Ilsung owner and their management. We know the Motors asset inside out. We have minimal diligence requirements. After all, we gave the license on the engine for the Chairman model. Yes?"

"Yes."

"We understand your client's priorities are certainty of closing and price, in that order, and we can provide certainty like no other—"

"They're all priorities."

Another silence. They're compelled to ask, "So, is there a path for Daimler to enter into negotiations with Ilsung or not?"

I could blow up the deal here. But that wouldn't be very sporting of me. "My client is open to all options."

"Give us a minute," he says, placing me on hold again.

I think about the promise I made to Wayne. Thunderball holds the keys to the kingdom, he said, gripping my shoulder. He gave me the project because he trusts me, and I promised to do my best to sell T-ball and salvage the group. I gave him my word. The image of the labor leader Yoon's earnest, unshaven face floats back to me. So too the bloodied, goggled head of the protester fallen next to me. The chant of the protesting laborers at the factory rings in my ears.

When he comes back on, Hesse says, "Can we assume there is a price at which Daimler will be granted exclusivity?"

Jack's strategizing returns to me; I know what he'd say. I remind myself, no bombs, have to make it seem plausible. "We're open to all options," I repeat.

"We need final sign-off from Stuttgart, but we are prepared to make a nonbinding offer of $1.95 billion in enterprise value, on a debt- and cash-free basis and assuming normal level of net working capital." He pauses for a reaction from me. Getting none, he continues, "That represents valuation of over seven times latest-twelve-months EBITDA. For exclusivity in negotiations. For the avoidance of doubt: if you insist on a competitive process, we are out." I can almost hear the umlaut.

It's a good price, higher than I expected and a decent premium to what the business is worth. Jack would've jumped at it. Uncharacteristic of the Germans. I begin to think maybe they're "pregnant," as we say, with the deal. They've decided they have to make this acquisition in Korea as a platform for expansion into China, a market with nearly unlimited potential. Or maybe, unbeknownst to us, management has committed to a deal with the Parks of Ilsung.

"Let me take it back to the client." Time for the slingshots. "One more thing," I say, with Detective Columbo–like casualness. "Daimler will need to assume the $4.5 billion in Ilsung Motors bank debt."

"Debt?" Hesse says. "We were guided that this was an asset sale? The tax implications for—"

"Stock deal. Debt goes with."

"We'll need to discuss it internally—"

"Also, there's unfunded pension liabilities, about $300 million." Now for the catapults. "Oh, and there's a few other contingent liabilities. Off-balance-sheet guarantees of sister Ilsung companies' loans, et cetera. Not a big amount, $500 million or so."

A stunned silence on the other end. I decide to go out guns blazing, like the North Korean commandos. "And we'll need ironclad job security for the employees, too."

"Job guarantees . . . that was never on the table—"

"It's a priority. For my client." For the avoidance of their doubt, I add, "It's a deal-breaker."

"This is . . . a lot to take in." They sound confused, defeated. "We'll need to discuss with senior management."

"You do that," I tell them. My insides feel fluttery, even as I tell myself, Make butterflies. In all the colors of the rainbow.

After hanging up, I consider calling Wayne to let him know I had a difficult discussion with Daimler and they may be on the way out. To tell him a deal, especially a complex sale, goes through ups and downs, *woo-yuh gok-jul*, kind of like the vicissitudes of life. I decide it's too late in Seoul, better to catch up with him in person later in the week.

Days of planning, hours of vacillating, and I've done it, shit-kicked Project Thunderball. I look at the doodles on my yellow pad. *Sabotage T-ball* → *Throw bombs? No, slingshots^^* → *High price bogey. Debt, contingents* → *Daimler out* → *No T-ball sale* → *Keep JOBS!! No cash for W/Ilsung to pay creditors* → *What happens to IS?!* Christ, what have I done?

Wayne will survive, I tell myself—that's what chaebol do. I'm doing the right thing. As Abuji counseled, and Jee Yeon suggested. But I will be alone with the consequences to carry with me.

Sitting in my father's chair, I survey the emptiness of the room, hollowed out of sound. The books around me, once so full of life and mystery and magic, look abandoned, forlorn; they could be blank as the books on Jay Gatsby's shelves. They're vessels without their master. The room a shrine with no purpose.

30

March 30, 1998

As I pass through the arrivals area at Gimpo, dizzy from another
sleepless fifteen-hour flight, a headline at the newsstand catches
my eye: ILSUNG TO DECLARE BANKRUPTCY. The article in *Daehan
Ilbo* details the imminent collapse of the Ilsung corporate empire.
Billed as the largest corporate bankruptcy in Korean history, at
$38 billion. I grab all the newspapers I can find and scramble into
a taxi.

News coverage of the Ilsung Group's mounting financial
troubles has been a building drumbeat for weeks. There were
reports of Ilsung Shipbuilding and Ilsung Construction missing loan payments. Speculation thrumming about how much
longer Corp. and Electron could continue propping up the
cash-hemorrhaging group affiliates. Pronouncements out of

the Blue House about an unwavering commitment to chae-bol reform. A couple of days ago, I saw footage of President DJ Kim proclaiming there would be no government bailout of Ilsung companies. Meaning only a market-based solution. Still, they said, this is the Republic of Chaebol. And Ilsung, *dae-ma bool-sa*. Big horse cannot die. Too large, too many jobs at stake.

Just before I left for Seoul, the Phipps coverage banker for Daimler-Benz had informed me of its intention to pull out of Thunderball. This intelligence should have made me feel gratified, but all I've been feeling is guilt and anxiety. I can't sleep, I have trouble breathing. I'm in Seoul to make sure GM Korea, the only viable remaining acquirer for Motors, also stays sidelined. The final nail. It has to be done, I reassure myself. Speed is of the essence now. *Sok-jun sok-gyul*, as Abuji taught me.

But an imminent group-wide bankruptcy is too quick for me, and beyond all my planning. Declaration of default at Electron or Motors would trigger cross defaults at many of the Ilsung companies and throw them into creditor-led workouts or court receivership. The fate of Motors and its workforce is up in the air. My T-ball gambit was a smart bomb, aimed at focused damage, not a nuclear bomb to blow up the group. I need to get things under control. I call Wayne from the taxi to get an update, also to check how much he knows, but I can't get him, not in his office, on his mobile, even his trusty beeper. Next I try the Group Strategy head, but no luck. I wonder briefly if they've found a back-channel arrangement with the government.

I riffle through the newspapers. There are pieces on the group flagships but not on Motors. The creditor group, in conjunction with the MoEP, is conducting a review of all the companies in the group to determine which entities it will take over, which to sell off, and which to put into court receivership or liquidation. The only done deals are KIDB takeovers of Ilsung Electron and Life Insurance. There are some articles on what might happen to Chairman Park and the owner family. An editorial in a liberal daily proclaims, "*Sah-pil kwee-jung.*" Justice prevails.

A right-leaning business daily runs a series of articles bemoaning the likely adverse impact of chaebol group failures and witch hunts of chaebol families on the economy and markets. The usual hand-wringing over a potential domino effect on other big groups. Just when the economy, struggling to recover, needs them the most. Not to mention the severe damage on the image of Korea abroad.

As soon as I reach my hotel room, I call Jack in the office. "A shit storm," he says, uncharacteristically solemn. "Might as well kiss T-ball goodbye. Monkey's sending the Restructuring team out from New York." A leading indicator of the beginning of the end.

"You okay?" Jack says. "You sound out of it."

"I gotta go," I say, closing the phone.

It's all getting ahead of me. No sooner do I hang up with

Jack than my phone rings—Jun this time. He says to turn on the TV.

I click to KBS, and the lead story is Wayne's father. Chairman Park has been charged with fraudulent accounting, tax evasion, and breach of fiduciary duty. An icon of Korean business, the face of chaebol power, in disgrace, goes the storyline. They run loop footage of a posse of prosecutors carting away boxes of documents and disembodied PCs from Ilsung's headquarters. Then they show Chairman Park in a wheelchair, wearing sunglasses and a face mask, being wheeled into Ilsung General Hospital. He's mobbed by reporters thrusting microphones in his face, shouting questions at him. He looks old, frail. He raises a weak hand to wave them off.

There's file footage of the Ilsung Group's sprawling global business empire. Black-and-white shots of Ilsung steel mills, more recent videos of Ilsung Electron DRAM chips and Ilsung LCD TVs spinning off assembly lines. The obligatory mention of the over forty business units and 280,000 employees.

Then I see it. The news crawl at the bottom of the screen: *KIDB-led creditor group to assume control of Ilsung Motors.* Thunderball gone.

Jun's voice comes crackling over the phone, left on the bed. "You seeing this? . . . You still there?"

A reporter comes on to say strategic discussions with "a leading German automaker" fell through at the last hour. Having no other prospects, the Motors creditors pulled the plug. The

Parks are out; KIDB and the creditors in. My foiling Daimler was the coup de grâce. Ilsung ran out of time. Just not the way I'd planned it.

I sit down on the bed. I picture the laborers of Motors, chanting their rights and fighting for their livelihood in the face of indignity and tear gas. Even if they keep their jobs for now, what will happen to them when the banks need to get their money back and put the company up for sale again? Did I really do right by them? I think of the Park family. Empire fallen, emperor to jail. What of the Prince? Wayne is probably in hiding somewhere, plotting his next move with Kim *Sil-jang*. Frantic is not his style; more like simmering resentment, at me for not being able to sell Motors to get him the desperately needed liquidity. Ruing ever trusting me. Guilt returns to me, crackling in the space between a flash of lightning and the clap of thunder to come.

I take a deep breath. It dawns on me that the scenario Wayne had been fearing was not his losing controlling power of Ilsung Group but the entire group's going under. This whole time he was trying to save the group. To salvage four decades of corporation building and some residual value for shareholders and bondholders, not to mention hundreds of thousands of jobs. And doing it the only way he knows how, exercising princely, unilateral control, however illicitly obtained. Like President Park Chung Hee, or Chun Doo Hwan after him, who each believed only he, wielding dictatorial powers, unconstitutionally secured, could lead the Republic to economic success. The grand delusion of monarchs and dictators alike, and their inevitable downfall. Wayne just didn't figure on his M&A adviser, and confidant, undermining him.

My BlackBerry twitches in vibration on the desk. I pick it up, and there are over twenty e-mails captioned "T-ball." A dozen urgent messages from M&A head Conway, saying, "Call me when you land," "Call right away," "CALL ASAP!!" I press down on the *off* button, bury the BlackBerry in my briefcase.

Just as I'm about to turn off the TV, there's breaking news. It's live footage of Wayne, his hands in handcuffs covered by a trench coat, being led into the General Prosecutor's office. His gait is lumbering, as if dragging his misdeeds behind him. Wayne's been charged with embezzlement, bribery of public officials, and tax evasion, more serious charges than his father's. Apparently, he tried to bribe the incoming secretary of civic affairs—a desperate ploy to "influence" the KIDB chairman to roll over the debt owed by the group. Wayne has on a baseball cap, and he keeps his eyes down even as he holds his head up.

As two prosecution officials lead him by the elbows to a spot for the press to take photos, a man with a red "United in Labor" bandanna rushes at Wayne. He hurls a bucket of what looks like cow dung at him. "Long live Ilsung Motors," he shouts, as he's wrestled away. A fireworks of popping flashbulbs as the Prince stands with shit dripping off his face.

I click off the TV. I lie down sideways on the bed.

An emperor without an empire. A business conglomerate out of cash, workers deprived of their jobs. A friendship robbed of trust. I think of Abuji. A life running out of breath.

31

March 31, 1998

It's a pale late winter afternoon. I walk outside my hotel to Nam-san Mountain, in the heart of Seoul. The saplings along a ridge are still wrapped in their corsets of straw, the boughs bare.

As I walk, I hold my breath, to feel what Abuji must be feeling. I want to know what it feels like to be running out of breath. When I asked him, Abuji said he felt faint, as if he'd spent hours blowing up balloons.

The sword of IPF, the Lee curse, has hung over my adult life. A giant gleaming sword dangling from some dark, remote place high above, ever threatening to fall, make its mortal plunge. Now that it's claimed Abuji, an abstract threat has the baldness of destiny for me.

A wind howls down from the top of the hills. A spectral sound, of moaning spirits.

Namsan is where Umma lost her parents and both her sisters. She told the story to Dongseng and me many times, adding layers of detail over the years. Summer of 1950, start of the 6.25 War, Umma would've been eleven when she was retreating with her family. The Democratic People's Liberation Army, in a surprise attack, had charged across the 38th parallel at dawn on Sunday, June 25, and rampaged through to Seoul. Within a few days of the North's invasion, the ill-prepared ROK Army lost 70,000 men of its 195,000-man force. By late June, it was in full retreat. The people of Seoul were forced to flee south toward Busan. Through her father's connections, Umma's family got a military escort.

On their refuge journey, they were told to take temporary shelter in a small cave on Namsan, then the southernmost part of Seoul. President Syngman Rhee and his cabinet had already been evacuated from Seoul, and after they crossed the Han River, they ordered the army to blow up the Hangang Bridge to stop the North Korean Army from crossing south. The destruction of the only bridge trapped hundreds of thousands of Seoul residents north of the river. That was why Umma's family had stopped, but they didn't know this when they were huddled in the cave, her father, mother, and two sisters, along with the army detail.

Umma was sharing a couple of rice balls her mother had prepared with her sisters. She remembers the sticky lotus leaf they were wrapped in, her mother's special touch. Out of nowhere, mortars whistled in and burst all around them. Umma says she remembers then only the concussive booms and the ensuing deafness. Everyone around her was hit, almost everyone fatally. When she came to her senses, she found her mother lying limply on top of her, having thrown herself on her youngest daughter to shield her from the incoming fire. She turned her mother over, and a crimson flower blossomed across her white silk *hanbok*.

Umma cradled her mother's head in her lap for hours before she was rescued. She nearly suffocated because the mouth of the cave was closed up from the debris. Her *unni*'s corpse was dug up with arms missing. They never found her twin sister's body. My mother was the sole survivor.

Later she learned it was friendly fire, the Americans. But Umma never blamed them, or President Rhee. It matters little who or how, she said. She wondered more about the why. Why her? She often said her twin sister was the good one; she's the one who should have lived. Why was her family killed, and why was she chosen to survive? Umma always ended the story with this question. A question that stayed with her, haunted her, over the years and decades.

Umma still has shrapnel lodged in her neck and stomach. When I was little, I used to trace my forefinger along the jagged edge of the shrapnel through her skin. The shrapnel moved a bit when I pressed it. The dulled sharpness of a pain past. Umma's own war mementos, which she carries around everywhere. She said they made her remember, always.

I search for the cave. Not expecting to find any answers but just to see for myself. But I can't find anything resembling a cave. There's a long staircase leading up to a large library and, farther up,

Namsan Tower. There are no remnants of battle amid the loamy earth. Still, I can sense it. There is violence and bloodshed and death buried in these hills. Souls entombed. Umma told us that on a still night, if you listen you can hear the muffled screams of anguish across Namsan. Ghosts of a cruel war that pitted brother against brother, son against father. Ghosts, too, of more recent warfare, waged by the torturers of the KCIA and its even more brutal successor Angibu on dissidents and student protesters in the 1970s and 1980s, right here in the bowels of these hills. How they wail, the ghosts of Korea's cursed history, in smothered lamentation. But I can't help feeling there is also redemption here. The sins of history not forgotten but, after all these years, maybe forgiven. Maybe that's what gives Namsan its forlorn beauty, an unspoken reconciliation with the past forged by time and nature.

I reach the top of Namsan, and the winds carry to me a premonition that my days are about to change in some wondrous way. I call Jee Yeon, whose voice, whispered, serene, is always a restorative. I don't say much, and neither does she, but it feels like enough for both of us.

32

Early April 1998

When I go to pick her up, Jee Yeon hurries out to meet me at the front gate, closing the heavy iron doors behind her. Beyond the gate, I glimpse a large, manicured garden, bonsai and cherry blossom trees, a front yard of enchantment, I imagine, and, higher up, a brick mansion, a rare sight in apartment-dense Seoul. A large *Taegukgi*, with the familiar red-blue yin and yang symbol, flutters in the wind.

I'm relieved not to face Chairman Chung again, but I wonder briefly if she's embarrassed to put me in front of her parents. It takes me a minute to realize it's the opposite.

"Embarrassed to show me your palace?" I say.

"*Anyoung* to you, too," she says, with a smile.

A garage door opens with a groan, and a shiny, black Chairman rolls out. The driver slides down the tinted glass window, asks, "Where to, *Agassi*?"

"*Anyo*, Ajussi, that's okay," she says, walking hurriedly past the sedan. "We'll just walk." She hooks her arm through mine and, as if lifting some of the heaviness I carry around, marches me forward in light steps.

"Looks like a nice car," I say, unable to resist. "Be a hell of a lot more comfy than one of those grubby taxis."

She pretends to ignore me.

"You know, denying your wealth is as silly as someone denying their poverty. You can't hide who you are. Besides, I don't care about that stuff."

"Well, it's not who I am," she says, in her usual quiet voice but with a firmness I'm not used to. "All that . . . that's Appa's. And soon to be Oppa's. Not mine."

"So, where," I say, changing the topic, "is this great stargazer?"

"In Miari. Short cab ride, if not too much traffic."

"Maybe we should take the bus. If we want to really do the proletarian thing." I get a laugh out of her. "Or ride bicycles there . . ."

"All right, all right," she says, hailing down a taxi.

In the taxi, she leans her head on my shoulder. "What's going to happen to your friend Hyun Suk?" she says. "And Ilsung?"

"I don't know what's in his stars," I say. "A chaebol without a company . . ." Better, I think, than a man without a country. "Going to visit him tomorrow. At the detention center."

"Poor your friend," she says and leaves it there. She and I both know the rest is up to me.

I roll down the window to get some air.

By the time we reach Miari, it's gotten dark. Under a rising amber moon, we walk around trying to find the place. We come to a run-down storefront with a placard on the door that says, in Chinese characters, CHULHAGWON. Literally, place of study of light, more commonly known as philosophy.

We open the door to a small room, and there is a man in his fifties, his long, white hair tied in a ponytail, sitting on the floor behind a low wooden desk. As if expecting us, he motions for us to sit. We sit on two red cushions on the floor in front of the desk. We tell him we're here to have our *koonghap* rendered.

The philosopher slides his horn-rim glasses down the nose and studies us, one, then the other. He asks for our vitals, on lunar calendar, as Jee Yeon had predicted. He wrinkles his nose when I tell him I don't know the hour of my birth.

The philosopher opens a thick, yellowed book, and the dust of centuries of wisdom floats up from it. He says, without looking up, "Western-educated?"

I nod.

"They've studied same thing in West through the ages," he says. "I don't mean astrology, horoscopes, I mean astronomy. 'Star regulating' in Greek. Greeks, then Romans, studied the stars and heavens to divine their future. It's all related." He brings his hands together, locks the fingers. "It's in Dante and Shakespeare. West, East. Same study.

"Of course, Western philosophers thought life moved linearly. That's why they focus, wrongly, on years, numbering them sequentially. The reality is, our lives go in cycles, like phases of the moon. The day, the months, the seasons, all go around and come back again. Life is a cycle."

The seer consults the charts in his book, traces our positions in them, his long forefinger a divining rod.

"You have to see the patterns based on what's happened before, over the centuries. Understand your position relative to the movements of celestial objects, the moon and the stars. Your fate is all there in the heavens."

He furrows his brow. "Your stars show there is too much shadow, not enough light," he says to me. "You have faced a great struggle. You have lost . . . a close friend." He watches me for a reaction. "Or rather, you will lose a relative." He sees me flinch and says, "A very close family member. Your mother."

I tilt my head skeptically. And he quickly adds, "Or your father."

Turning to Jee Yeon, he says, "You fight your stars. You fought them. But they're moving . . . moving toward you. Your fire energy used to be excessive, but now is coming more into balance with your water. Now you accept."

She listens impassively.

"In the old days, because of your fire-water imbalance, you might have had problems with your uterus. Now, you will be able to conceive. I see . . . a son."

Enough of our *saju*, Jee Yeon says. "What of our compatibility?"

The philosopher-seer flips pages back and forth. "Strangely enough, your stars line up. Your own imbalances are compensated by the other's. Your fire energy mixes well with his earth energy. You each have your, ah, issues, but together, you over-come them."

He looks up. "I see harmony in your union. You are . . . a felic-itous match."

Before he can elaborate, I thank him and give a vigorous bow. I put down a few bills on the desk, and I take Jee Yeon's hand and rush out the door.

We've barely reached the alleyway outside when we burst out laughing. Our laughter comes back down the alleyway as the sound of applause. We feel a release, a liberation of some momentous sort, and, like a ripe peach splitting, an opening of possibilities before us.

"That's it then," I say when I catch my breath. "Our union is blessed by the heavens. *Felicitous.*"

"It's meant to be," she says. "I can tell my parents."

"Just out of curiosity, what would you have done if the reading hadn't been auspicious?"

"Taken us to the next star reader. And then the next."

I can only smile.

We walk in quiet for a few blocks.

"The moon and the stars are lining up for us," I say. "I think that's what they call destiny."

"Our destiny, Dae Joon-*ssi.*"

"You know, if you like, we could just leave." I turn to look at her. "My work here is over. Sovereign bond done deal, M&A deal, well, gone. We could go to Germany."

"Deutschland," she says, rolling the name around her tongue like a *satang*, hard candy.

"Always wanted to go. Can always come back here in the future, of course."

"We could do that," she says. And she takes my hand in hers.

The rapturous cry of an infant from above pierces the quiet of the alley. Under the iridescent moonlight, in the rippling beauty of Jee Yeon's eyes, the ghosts of the past are extinguished, the superstitions, even the curse, lifted, and the promise of a future with its hopes and dreams is given miraculous birth.

33

April 1998

The detention center where they house Wayne is in Uiwang, an hour southwest of Seoul. It has the barbed wire outside and the bare cinder-block walls you'd expect. A buzz, a release-opened door, and a bare room with a desk and two chairs. There's a guard, his face a gargoyle, sitting in the back, taking notes.

Wayne comes in and gives me a wan smile. His hair is unmoussed, his face unshaven. He wears a tan inmate uniform that looks large on him.

Before I can ask, Wayne says, "Holding up fine, pardner."

Usually when I'm with wealthy people, even Jee Yeon, I feel guilt in the air, but I've never felt that way with Wayne. He knew wealth was his lot, and he was comfortable with it and trying to tend it and grow it. But now he's different. His corporate kingdom gone, his *Sil* dismantled, Wayne seems lost. I don't see disappoint-ment or anger in his face. What I see is confusion. It wasn't meant to be this way. His belief in the universe has been shaken to its core.

"Food okay?" I hardly know what else to ask.

"Vegetables and rice," he says. "Barley rice. Temple food. Like the North Koreans. Good way to lose weight." He pats his flat-tened stomach. He offers, "Sorry about Thunderball."

Words catch in my throat. I've been racked with the thought that my T-ball gambit with the Germans started the chain of events that landed Wayne here, in jail. His misplaced apology is an accidentally sprouted dandelion in a weed garden of secrets and lies.

"At least I didn't blow a real million in a squash match," I manage to say. "They treating you okay, otherwise?"

"Guards leave me alone. Other people here, well, this is white-collar detention, so I know many of them." He finds this amusing. "One thing in here, you have a lot of time."

"You doing any painting?" I say.

He shakes his head. "They don't let me. Art is apparently not a good statement of repentance. Warden said this is not a resort. You're not here on vacation."

I shake my head.

"I have time to think," he says. "I meditate a lot."

I wait for more, a revelation of some realization he's made, a hint of regret perhaps. But none is forthcoming. That wouldn't be Wayne.

"So. Been on any dates?" he says, brightening. "Some hot new talent?"

"Actually, I've been seeing someone," I say. "She's a musician, a cellist."

"Is it serious?" He lifts his eyebrows. "Meet her parents yet?"

"Yeah. Her father's kind of scary."

"Sounds pretty serious."

"It is. She brings out something in me. Think the good part."

"Just make sure she brings out the Hanguk *nom* in you."

"We're making . . . plans. Actually, I think you know her. She knows you."

"Small society." He's used to people knowing him. "Let's hope I get out in time for the wedding."

Wayne has been indicted for embezzlement, bribery, and tax evasion. And the General Prosecutor's Office has added perjury to his list of felonies. He's now in a liminal state, waiting for his next incarnation as he awaits trial. If convicted, he faces up to seven years in prison, although chaebol chieftains often have their sentences commuted, supposedly for the good of the economy.

"Heard you hired Chang & Kim," I say.

"Yeah, best law firm money can buy. But I'm not intending to fight."

"You're cooperating?"

"I don't see how Abuji could survive prison, at his age," he says, by way of explanation. "One of us has to go. My lawyers say I play the ball, they go easy on the old man."

It's the first time I've heard Wayne refer to the chairman as his *abuji*. Wayne sounds like he's made up his mind to fall on the sword, for his father.

"But surely you could contest some of the charges?"

Wayne looks at the guard, then lowers his voice. "They've got a lot of shit on us. The dirty dry cleaning." He adds, "From Dongseng."

"Kane?" I say. His younger brother blew the whistle? He must have turned state's witness.

"He sold Ajussi up the river," Wayne says.

Almighty No. 2 down, just like that. "The pressure must've gotten to Kane—"

"You don't understand. He'd *planned* it." He sees incomprehension on my face. "It was his revenge. Getting back at me. For getting the throne. At Abuji, too."

"Hard to believe . . . your little brother could do that."

"He claimed he wanted to clean up the group, to start a new Ilsung." He shakes his head. "Of course, he just wanted it for himself. *Ttolai* had no idea what kind of trouble we were in—real trouble, I mean. The financial mess. He thought with me out of the way, he'd be crowned king and inherit the group as it was. Well, *après moi, le deluge*.

"Worst part is Abuji," he continues. "After all Abuji has done for him, for us . . ."

Wayne looks defeated. I don't know if he has true remorse for what he did or whether he even did what he's charged with. I sense he thinks it all unfair, his getting singled out for punishment when all the chaebol heads do the same deeds, have done it for years. What hurts is Kane's betrayal. His father must have felt it, too. Is there a deeper cut than defeat by your own flesh and blood? Family betrayal, that's against the order of the universe.

"Abuji collapsed when he found out," he says. "I hear he's stopped eating since he learned I'm preparing to go serve time." He sounds broken.

I take a deep breath, say, "I have something to tell you, too."

Wayne looks up at me. His face is not one that can bear more pain. But he needs to know, and he deserves to hear it from me. And I need to tell him.

"Thunderball . . . it may not be what it seemed," I say. "The truth is, I led Daimler astray, when they had serious interest. I . . . I blew up the deal." Is it another form of selfishness, I wonder, to confess to someone to alleviate your own conscience? My confession is a thief, taking away more than it gives.

"How?" He looks confused. "Why would you do that?"

"I let Daimler and the other buyers know about the contingent liabilities and made jobs guarantee a closing condition. I went against your interests, I did wrong by you as a client and a friend, and by my firm. To do what I thought was right."

"Which was?"

"To save lives. Thousands of workers would have been out on the street. So I did what I could to make sure that didn't happen."

All Wayne says is, "I should've known. Ever the idealist. Champion of the people."

"I'm sorry . . . Truly sorry."

He closes his eyes. "So did it? Save jobs?"

"I think so. We don't know what will happen with the creditors and the court receiver. But I like to think I've given the workers a fighting chance." I leave out *and free from chaebol oppression.*

A heavy quiet hangs between us.

"I suppose it doesn't matter now," he says, sighing. "Even if Daimler had moved ahead, who knows if the deal would have gone through. Or if T-ball would have saved the group, overcoming . . . all the other stuff."

Wayne's charity makes it worse. Anger is easier than understanding; it's a shelter you can hide in. I expected, maybe even wanted, him to explode in anger and hurt, to condemn me as the worst kind of human being, one who turns on a friend. I certainly deserve it. But in his quiet forgiveness, he's left it to me to forge my own peace.

In the waning late afternoon light, Wayne looks emaciated. His tan shirt hangs too loosely on his shrunken frame. "You should make sure to eat," I tell him. "Keep up your strength."

"Interferes with my meditation. I'm trying to dissolve space into light." He smiles weakly. "Before entering the next stage."

I've read about the self-mummifying Buddhist monks. To ensure passage to the next bardo, the monk would lock himself in a small stone tomb underground, where, sitting in the lotus position, he would meditate and recite mantras. His only connection with the outside world was a bamboo tube, through which he'd breathe. It typically took a thousand days for the monk to attain the goal of bodily desiccation, which disassociated his soul from physical body. This would allow it to travel toward a blissful reincarnation.

Five more minutes, says the guard.

"Crazy thing in all this?" Wayne says. "I didn't even want to be Ilsung chairman." He runs his hands through his hair, an old habit. "I never asked for this. I was just doing my duty as *jangnam*."

The shared fate of first sons in Korean families. A right of birth that somewhere along the line turns into a duty that, in turn, becomes the burden of a lifetime. So much weight, too much weight; some of us learning to accept and bear it, others getting crushed under it.

"You're a good son," I say.

"Not good enough," he says. "How's your *buchin*?"

"Abuji's in the hospital, too. I'm going back to New Jersey tomorrow. He may not have much time left."

"Anything I can do to help?" he says reflexively, and we both find ourselves laughing at the absurdity and sadness of his offer, though his laugh is without the trademark peals of thunder.

"I want to spend his last days with him," I say.

"You're a good son, too. A *hyoja* . . . Isn't it strange to think we're going to be fatherless someday?"

My breath stops. *Fatherless.* The Earth falls away under my feet. To be a son without a father. Alone. Lost. Terror. Eternity.

I agree it is, strange, and sad. And I leave him with a fierce, wordless hug.

34

November 1999

At *gijesa* for Abuji, Umma gives me a gift of time.

It's been a year since Abuji's passing, and our family is gathered for the anniversary memorial service. Korea has recovered from what Koreans have taken to calling the IMF Crisis. The government paid off its $21 billion loan from the International Monetary Fund two years ahead of schedule. The banks have been recapitalized, with both state funds and foreign private capital, and industry is back on its feet. Ilsung Group is no more, though its consumer electronics products are still sold under the Electron name. Ilsung Motors was sold by the creditors to a Chinese automaker at a fire-sale price but on condition of job security for all employees. Wayne served his time, nine months in prison, the remaining four years commuted. The Prince now lives in exile. He's in Silicon Valley, his new incarnation venture capital. I suggested the name Ozymandias Ventures.

Jee Yeon and I got married in a traditional ceremony in New Jersey. For my father's sake, we skipped the engagement. Abuji attended the wedding in a wheelchair with an oxygen tank, in what would be his last outing in public. Umma looked beatific in her blue *hanbok*, a gift from her daughter-in-law. Minister Choi, now Uncle, presided as *jurye*. In a benediction sprinkled with recycled wisdom from the classics, he exhorted us to obey our parents and follow our hearts.

I left Phipps a little over a year ago. It was to spend Abuji's last days with him. But I never went back. I haven't been able to leave finance altogether, but at least I can count my days of autoasphyxiation by necktie behind me. Purpose doesn't come in sharp rays of sunlight, but a ripe dusky light guides my work most days.

We live in Berlin, my wife and I. From a divided country to a once-divided city, riven no more. There are ghosts here, too. We were brought here by music, the Berlin Philharmonic, which had offered Jee Yeon a position. We stayed because we've found haunting beauty in the parks, the weeping trees of Tiergarten, the grim art galleries and the Weimar-era cafés. The unshaven, unbathed, dirty-jeaned Berliners have welcomed us with their large hearts. One stormy day, we walked along the Berlin Wall, and under the lightning the crumbled, graffiti-laced facade and the cracked tombstones of concrete seemed to sink into the ground. It's a city of guilt and remorse, but with a soul redeemed by a reconciliation with its past.

The year Abuji passed away, my son Tae was born. A cosmic symmetry, a yin and yang of loss and gain, that was meant to give me solace somehow but seemed only cruel. Abuji barely had any strength left when I put tiny, bundled Tae in his arms. There were dark puddles of indeterminable depth in Abuji's eyes, recognizing, then unrecognizing. *Sonja,* Umma told him. *Your grandson.* A life lived, a story already told, another beginning.

We buried Abuji's body at Eunsan. We made the long climb up the family mountain, and I introduced Jee Yeon and Tae to Ajussi. He held baby Tae in his arms, and they smiled tooth-less smiles at each other. We put up a new marble marker at the ancestral burial site, bearing the *hanja* characters of Abuji's name. I saw there was room for a few more tombs, and I took solace in knowing where my final destination will be. My final home.

Before we begin the *jesa* ceremony, Umma hands me a small silk *bojagi.* Inside, there is Abuji's old Patek chronograph. I can't breathe. I hold the watch in my hand, stare at it for a long time before I put it on. The familiar small gold-trimmed face, the brown leather strap, a bit frayed. I put it around my left wrist, the way he used to. I wind the dial—feed it rice, as Korean say—and the golden long hand moves.

"A reminder," Umma says. She doesn't say of what, and she doesn't need to. The spectral piano music, the political discus-sions, the playing catch, the laughs, the walks, the things said and unsaid, the hurt, disappointment, understanding, and forgiveness, all of it, the moments and the entire timeline, is remembered. *He wanted you to have it.* Dongseng watches wordlessly, wiping away tears running down her cheek.

The *jesa* shrine is set with the *byungpoong*, our family screen passed down through generations, facing north. The food is laid out in prescribed order on a lacquer table. A bowl of rice and plates of beef *galbi*, three kinds of colored vegetables and white fruits, set back to front, on the side facing west; taro soup, *goolbi*, and red fruits, sliced open at the top, on the east. Dongseng has added a plate of Teuscher chocolate truffles, Abuji's favorite, in the front row. Two white candles are placed at opposite ends of the table and a portrait of Abuji at the center in back. He presides over the proceedings with his beneficent, knowing eyes.

Abuji's love was the gentlest love I've known, and the love ended a year ago. Expectation, hope, and, yes, probably disappointment, but in the end, all was washed away, cleansed, by overwhelming love. The love born of acceptance. Grief for Abuji comes in waves, and the waves come still.

There is now only peace. As the Hindus have recited through the ages, and as T. S. Eliot distilled in one crystal moment, *Shanti, Shanti, Shanti.* Peace in the world, peace with the divine, and, most exalted, peace within. Internal peace doesn't come all at once, overwhelming you like a tsunami. Peace comes in drops. Like drops from an IV drip bag, slowly, one small drop at a time. And you learn to take it when it comes. You receive the drops of peace with both hands, accept them in gratitude and with humility. Before you know it, your hands are full and peace is yours. *Shanti.*

By custom, *chohun*, the initial offering, is performed by the *jangnam*. Koreans call the eldest son of the deceased a *jwein*, sinner. The sin is of having survived the parent. I kneel, light the incense, pour *cheongju*, rice wine, in a cup and circle the cup three times over the incense sticks. I do the ritual bow twice, touching my forehead to the floor, followed by the women, Umma, Dongseng, and Jee Yeon, bowing four times. Umma reminds us we honor not only Abuji, but five generations of ancestors before him. His spirit is but the latest in a conjoined line of Lee spirits.

We celebrated Tae's *dol*, his first birthday, a month ago. We invited our relatives and friends, and we had the traditional feast and a photo session. Everyone said how nice the picture of Umma with Tae was; I saw only the empty space where Abuji would have been. At the end of the ceremony, we watched Tae choose among a spool of thread, a ten-thousand-won bill, and a pencil laid out on a table. Tae picked up the pencil in his tiny fist. The newest candidate to succeed a long line of scholars. They said how proud his grandfather would have been.

I serve the main offering, laying a spoon in the rice bowl and metal chopsticks on the *goolbi*. We open the back door so the spirits of Abuji and the ancestors may come to receive the offerings and partake in the meal. There's a moment of silence for the spirits to eat in peace and quiet. We end the *jesa* by bowing twice, bid the spirits a good journey back home.

As we gather at the table to eat the *jesa* food, Umma lifts Tae in her arms and says, *Jangson*, eldest son of eldest son. Continuing after me the long lineage of Lee men. It will be his duty to carry on the sacred family tradition. Maybe he will become a wise *sunbi* scholar. Maybe he will outlive the curse.

I look in Tae's eyes, and I see, as every parent before me has seen, the beginning and the end of all questions. This little bundle of gurgles and pains will grow to know anguish and suffering and joy. He will struggle even as he learns and creates. But he will one day feel love in his heart. His insistent yearning for happiness and redemption contains all the answers of the universe. In his will to live and grow lie the length and breadth and weight of all philosophy, Plato's meaning of forms, Kierkegaard's leap, Confucius's secular as sacred. From our ancestors to Abuji to me to my *adeul*. Through the roar of destiny and the hiss of curse. The flow of life, in all its rage and anguish and mystery and ceaseless wonder.

Acknowledgments

As with most first-time novelists, I owe a debt of gratitude to many people. My wife, Kyung Ah, was with me every step of the way, from conception to thinking through plot and character points. She gave me advice when I sought it; and time and space when I needed that, even if it meant forgoing weekends and vacations. My sister, Mimi, provided valuable guidance on narrative matters as well as unwavering encouragement from beginning to end. She had more faith in this book than I ever did. Without their support, *Offerings* would not be what it is.

I feel blessed to have found an editor in Cal Barksdale who "got" my writing and put his brilliant red pen to work in his distinctively gentle way. Working with him was like dancing the tango with an old, familiar partner. His editorial suggestions made *Offerings* immeasurably better. I am grateful to the Arcade/Skyhorse publisher, Tony Lyons, for taking a chance on a debut novel. And thanks to my agents at Creative Arts Agency, David Larabell and Michael Gordon, who believed in me.

I also wish to thank several early readers of the book. Theresa Park, Lorin Stein, Jong Ha Yoon, and Eliot Bu all provided helpful comments. In researching the finance-related background of the book, I found corroboration of my notes in various articles in *Euromoney* and *FinanceAsia*. I also found welcome reminders of traditional Korean tales and scenes from my childhood in the books on Korea by Tuttle Publishing and Hollym.

Lastly, my *umma*, of course. For a lifetime of sharing stories, including the most powerful one, her own.